DARK

James A. Brakken

Author of

The Treasure of Namakagon

TheTreasureofNamakagon.com

Enter with caution:

Here there be dragons.

DARK

ISBN-13: 978-0615698533 ISBN-10: 0615698530

Badger Valley Publishing

BadgerValley.com
45255 East Cable Lake Road
Cable, Wisconsin 54821
BayfieldCountyLakes@Yahoo.com

Other than Chief Namakagon, no characters in this book represent actual individuals. Any similarity to real persons, either living or dead, is unintentional and coincidental. Unlike the text, all images that follow are copyright free. They are meant not to illustrate the writings but to add mystery and visual relief to the poems and stories.

The author expresses sincere gratitude to the gifted authors in the Yarnspinners Chapter of the Wisconsin Writers Association for their steadfast support and creative counsel.

"Deep into that darkness peering,
long I stood there,
wondering,
fearing,
doubting,
dreaming dreams no mortal
ever dared to dream before."

Edgar Allen Poe

DARK

James A.
Brakken

Table of Contents:

Thief of Dreams

From dusk to dawn he wanders through your town,
Hour after hour,
Haunted by his power,
A dark gift he once tried to lay aside.
But, since his mentor died,
He's relished in this strange equation.
He can invade the mind of anyone,
A one-way conversation,
Reading any dreams that linger there.

A loner he'd become, this pitiful lad.
His mentor, it now seems,
Also purloined dreams.
But now this curse was his and his alone.

One starlit night a drunkard lay just down your road.
That's where our boy
Explored his most-loved joy
Of delving into nightmares, dark and deep.
While the man did sleep
Our lad explored the strangest visions.
Visions black but true,
Satan's favorite view.
Hence, this book before you did unfold.

2012, James A. Brakken, author of The Treasure of Namakagon, BadgerValley.com

A heavy load this drunkard carried in his mind.
Each refrain
Wrought him fear and pain
As frightful dreams streamed through his sleeping brain.
Yet, our boy remained,
Drinking in the old man's nightmares.
Ignoring every warning,
Absorbing death and mourning,
Seeking out the darkest dreadful tale.

Now, like the Thief of Dreams this boy'd become,
You, dear one, have just begun
A journey down this dreary track.
You can't turn back.
There is no stopping at the station.
A voyeur are you now
Of nightmares. Oh, and how
You'll dread the turn of each and every page.

Clarence Walter Wilson's Nest Egg

"Make yourself at home, Clarence. Lillian should be here directly. Pour yourself a drink."

That upstairs shout came from Henry Warburton, my fiancée's bull-like father. As usual, I followed his orders. Imported brandy—a luxury during Prohibition. I slammed it and poured another full tumbler.

Warburton's damn trophies littered the mantle. He was best of the best in pistol marksmanship. One-by-one, I scrutinized his precious awards. That's when I spotted the envelope neatly tucked behind the family portrait. I peeked inside—five one-hundred-dollar bills. I swiftly replaced it when the front door opened.

"Clarence?"

"In here, Darling."

Lillian Warburton was sweet, savvy, a living doll. We wanted so to marry but the old bull insisted I first have financial stability. I was out of work—in 1932.

She dropped her books. We embraced.

I poured my third bandy.

"Clarence, have you considered Daddy's advice?"

"Lillian, I'll find work soon. We'll get by. I'll …"

"Clarence! You heard Daddy. We *must* wait until we can afford our own life. I will not accept living with my parents once we wed."

We had other words.

Angry, I left, door slamming, another fifth of Henry's brandy in my coat pocket.

I retuned around midnight, by flashlight, I broke in through his kitchen door. I found my way to the parlor, the mantle, the envelope—our nest egg! Miss Lillian Marie Warburton and Mister Clarence Walter Wilson could now marry.

"Who's there!" Henry shouted.

I spun toward the stairway.

My flashlight blinding him, he fired.

I slumped.

The old bull knelt over me.

"My God, Clarence. I didn't know it was you. My God. My God. What—what's this?"

He tore the envelope from my hand.

"Clarence Wilson, you fool! Why, oh why, would you steal your own damn wedding gift? Oh, Clarence, you fool."

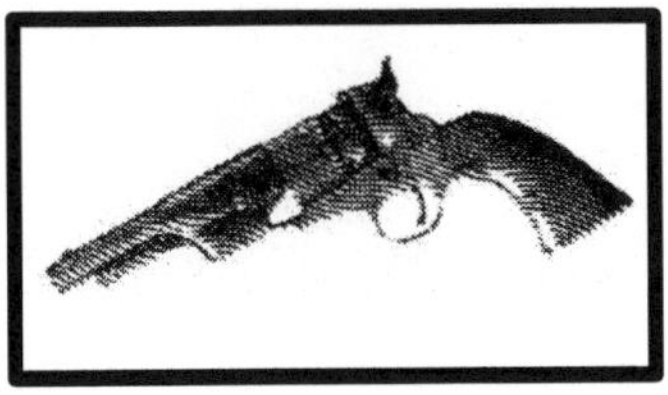

2012, James A. Brakken, author of The Treasure of Namakagon, BadgerValley.com

Beyond Superstition Creek

Somewhere up on a stream
Known as the Superstition,
Beyond the swamp where Oscar Morey died,
I tried my luck a-fishin'.
With a swish my hand-tied fly
Flashed above the pool,
Landing gently on the other side.

It floated there, while, just below,
A Brookie eyed it briefly,
Then broke the surface with a fearsome smash.
My hand-tied fly it did grasp
'Fore dashing down so deep.
Then, flashing to the surface,
It crashed the evening silence with a splash.

All my concentration
Focused fishward now.
So, I did not see old Oscar's ghost down there.
To him, did I appear like
Some hand-tied fly? Oh, my!
This creek called Superstition we now share.

2012, James A. Brakken, author of The Treasure of Namakagon, BadgerValley.com

Now, somewhere there's a pool
Where Brookies often school.
Giant trout, waiting there to thrill.
Superstition Creek it's said,
Will ne'er give up its dead,
When Oscar's ghost makes yet another kill.

And where is this Superstition?
That's not for you to know.
Go there not, dear angling friend of mine.
Danger lurks in waters cool.
Tread thee not there or, like this fool,
You'll be on the end of Oscar Morey's line.

Bedmates

A blood-thirsty spider resides
Close by in the dark. And, besides,
Because of your hair,
It's warmer down there.
'Twixt pillow and mattress he hides.

The Parson Joshua Black

You'll all be damned!" he shouted out.
"Condemned to burn in hell!
Unless you climb high on the hill
And fill your hearts so dark,
With prayerful words, oh, sinners you.
Now pack your bags and go.
Go seek out God's glory there.
Where the angels stay. They know
All you've done in your meek life
Wife and husband, daughter, son,
'Tis time your journey was begun.
Go ye now, high up the mound,
And lay thee down your burden there.
Carry forward. Do not wait.
Or never reach ye, Heaven's gate.

And so he led the people there,
Upon the fair and gentle hill.
Until the Prince of Darkness,
Thrilled to see them all,
Called to the congregation,
"Come and dance with me.
Dance the never ending dance,
Dance until you're free."

2012, James A. Brakken, author of The Treasure of Namakagon, BadgerValley.com

The sinners soon all shed their clothes
and danced the night away.
And, by the bright October moon
The Devil's tune was played.
The preacher tried to reign them in,
Save these sinners from such sin
As no man ever saw before.
I saw it all. I'll say no more.

The parson stood and shouted now,
"You must stop!" Oh, but how
These sinners simply loved their sinning so.
They shared whiskey from the jug
And, dancing to this evil drug,
Abandoned all their will and let it go.

This preacher watched in disbelief,
His grief was plain to see.
He'd have to find a way to free
His people from this curse.
Seeking other tactics now,
He took old Satan by the horn
And warned him not to stand in Heaven's way.

Captured, Satan had no choice.
His voice it echoed in the night.
"Parson Black, I beg you, please give way.
I will let your people go.
Just give to me your mortal soul."
"Never," cried the preacher, "will I stray."

The Prince of Darkness laughed out loud,
From somewhere there beneath his shroud.
"I'll have you now or later, Parson Black.
Come back with me to my domain
And reign above my field of pain
And suffering. Why, you'd be like a king!

Come with me, oh Joshua Black.
Turn your back on these wretched souls.
They'll never thank you for this stand you make.
Live the grand and glorious life.
Every night another wife.
Every day lay sleeping in the sand.
You'll sit beside me on a throne.
It seems so simple to decide.

What have these sinners ever done for you
But cause you worry and concern?
Turn to me. Earn respect
From each new soul that I collect.
Release me now and power you shall earn."

And this is where the story ended.
The congregation soon descended,
Tired and naked, shiv'ring in the cold.
They told of fire, pain, and grief
And of relief they finally gained
When Satan told them all they could go home.

From that day they stayed the path,
Wrath of Satan never doubting,
Pious to the core, through and through.
Only one did not come back,
The former parson, Joshua Black,
Who sits upon his throne awaiting you.

2012, James A. Brakken, author of The Treasure of Namakagon, BadgerValley.com

Thief of Dreams II

Now I urge you, muster all your courage.
Another leaf
You need to turn,
But only after you confirm
The door is barred.
For if not locked,
No blocking of nightmares frightful
Will protect you from another night
Full of fear and terror.

Turn the leaf, I dare.

The Zombie Apocalypse

The formula worked—well, somewhat. It was my third attempt with this particular solution. I was confident it would stimulate tissues back to life. It had worked on the neighbor's cat and a few squirrels that found themselves caught in my live trap before I drowned them. The squirrels seemed fine after the injection brought them back to life. The cat? Well, it was alive—but not quite the same as before. I heard my neighbor comment that it seemed disoriented. Disoriented and particularly hungry—not for its normal kibble, but for mice and birds—carnivorous behavior their cat had not previously displayed. Her words made me ponder how my solution would have affected Wilbur, her beagle.

Yes, my formula worked—on small animals. But would it work on humans? There was only one way to determine this and it was neither legal nor moral. On the other hand, if I succeeded, think of the good it could do for medicine—for Mankind! My God, imagine the possibilities!

Around eleven that evening, I found myself wandering with a solution-filled syringe in hand near the San Francisco waterfront. I believed I could find some wayward drunk, some societal reject, who would… well, let's say, "cooperate" in my experiment. It didn't take long. I found my subject under Pier 7 at the east end of Broadway. He looked to be about thirty-five to forty, though maybe younger. Some lifestyles make it difficult to judge age. He was drunk, all right. Out cold. I had no problem administering the plastic bag over his head and securing it and his hands with duct tape. He hardly struggled, then lay there, motionless. I checked for a pulse. When quite certain he had expired, I injected my solution directly into his heart with a four-inch cul-de-sac needle.

I waited. Five, ten, twenty minutes. He didn't come around. I tried chest compressions. Nothing. I went home, depressed and dejected, vowing to keep working on my formula until I had a viable solution.

The next morning I was in my neighborhood coffee shop when I saw the KNTV News item crawl across the bottom of the TV screen: TWO LONGSHOREMEN DEAD AFTER WATERFRONT DISMEMBERMENT. SFPD DENIES MIDNIGHT DEATH CAUSED BY ZOMBIE. I didn't pay much attention—all part of this ridiculous Zombie Apocalypse craze I supposed.

That's when my neighbor stopped in—the woman with the cat? She was really down. Seems her beagle died last night. Poor, poor Wilbur. Her cat had killed it. Ate all but the bones.

Drink your milk

An invisible troll named O'Toole
Sits back in your fridge on a stool.
You won't know what's up
Till you tip up your cup
And find on the bottom, troll drool.

Three Dragons

The First Dragon

Having never before killed a dragon, I was, to say the least, unprepared for what happened when I found myself seeking not one, but three. It was not my idea. The King of Fairland by the Sea had decreed he would give the hand of his daughter in marriage, to the first subject delivering to him severed dragon heads, the grisly proof of the three beasts' demise. His Majesty's daughter, mind you, was an only child. Thus, with said marriage, would come the entire kingdom one day—a fine kingdom made all the better by ridding it of these three troublesome creatures. Seven others had tried but failed to slay the trio of malevolent, revolting monsters. All seven of these brave men were now missing—dead, I supposed. I entered the cave, my sword at the ready.

"Who dares trespass?" came a gravelly voice through the musty dark.

"Only a friend of the slain to gather their remains for burial, Sir Dragon," I replied.

"Come closer then and I will show you the way to what's left of your comrades."

As I stepped into the darkness toward the raspy voice, I caught the whiff of the beast's hot, vile breath and my heart pounded. With a sudden, violent flapping of its leathery wings, the dragon leapt at me. I instinctively thrust my sword high, more in defense than offense, and was astonished when the giant creature impaled itself on my outstretched weapon. Bright orange blood gushed from its pierced throat. The dragon's razor-sharp teeth missed my face by mere inches as it fell dead at my feet. I soon severed head from neck, wiped the orange, viscous fluid from my sword, and lashed the grisly proof of my first slain dragon to my belt. One dead, two more to conquer, I advanced into the cold, dark, musty cave.

A Bedtime Story

"There's nothing underneath the bed.
Rest your eyes," my granny said.
"Nothing lurking there for you.
Don't be scared, my dearest.
Your fear is based on make believe.
Now leave such thoughts behind.
Find kinder dreams like fields of sheep.
There's nothing underneath the bed.
Sleep, my child. Sleep."

She doused the candle, closed the door,
And soon I heard beneath the floor,
A muffled voice. No choice had I
But to peek below.
I had to know what, from the black,
Might attack and leave me dead.
Still, I heard my granny's words,
"There's nothing underneath the bed.
Sleep, my child. Sleep."

Somewhere there, below my room,
Gloomy bones lay in the soil
And ragged tissues rotted.
Not an inkling did I have
Who or what or when.
Again it came, that rasping moan.
Granny was wrong when she said,
"There's nothing underneath the bed.
Sleep, my child. Sleep."

Weeping now, from fear and dread,
The trap door I swung open wide
And spied below, by candlelight,
A corpse there in the dirt.
He grinned at me, or so it seemed,
By the flick'ring light.
Was this a dream? My granny'd said,
"There's nothing underneath the bed.
Sleep, my child. Sleep."

Its bony hand then snatched me down.
The trap door slammed behind,
Binding me within its arms.
A prison most obscene,
I tried to scream and stop this dream.
But only Granny heard my cry.
It seems she lied each time she said,
"There's nothing underneath the bed.
Sleep, my child. Sleep."

Now, as you lay you down to sleep
And pray the Lord your soul to keep,
And wonder if your soul He'll take,
If you should die, before you wake,
Think of me below.
And know that if you lift the door,
Nevermore will it be said,
"There's nothing underneath the bed.
Sleep, my child. Sleep."
Now, sleep, my child. Sleep.

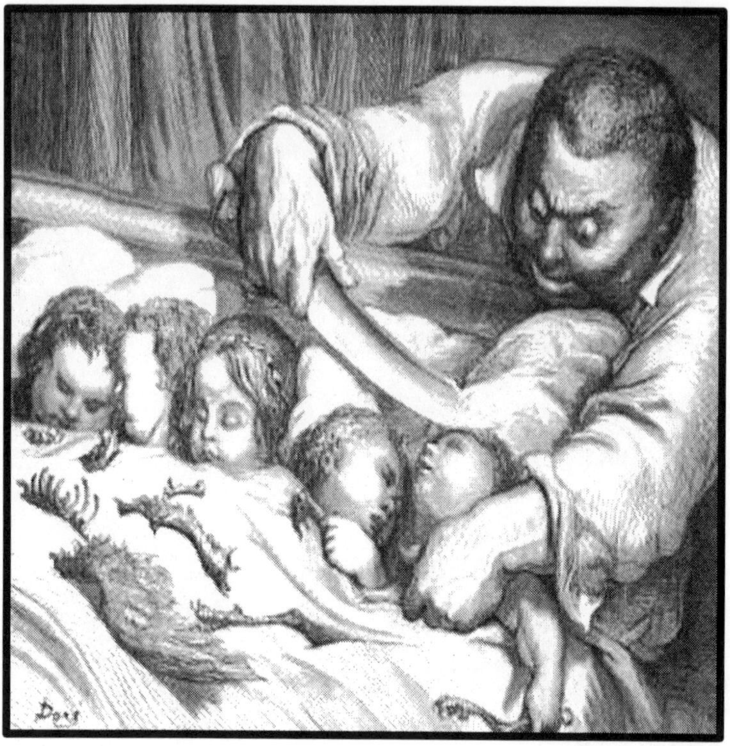

The Count

Dare not from his dark heart remove that stake.
Dare not grant him life, for mercy sake.
Swear to all that you will find a way
To keep him in his tomb till judgment day.

Dare not increase for all this deadly bane.
Dare not upon this land release such pain.
Make now a pledge to let the demon stay
Deep within his tomb till judgment day.

Dare not let him succeed in his dark deed.
Dare not allow him to proceed, I plead.
Make now an oath that you will e'er obey
To keep him in his tomb till judgment day.

Dare not grant him life, for mercy sake.
Dare not from his dark heart remove that stake.

Dark Visions

(Excerpt from THE TREASURE OF NAMAKAGON

We know what we have left behind. The great mystery lies beyond the next bend.

Each stroke of the Indian chief's paddle was strong and steady. His canoe glided silently along the shore, leaving only a gentle wake. He headed westward along Lake Superior's southern shore, not knowing where his journey would end—a journey that began with a dark, dark vision.

It was September, 1831. Weeks before, he was in the best graces of Major Lewis Wilson Quimby, commander of the United States Army post at Sault Ste. Marie on the eastern end of Lake Superior. An Ojibwe scout in his younger days, the chief contracted with the United States government to explore and map the many islands in Lake St. Claire and the forests far to the north. The Ojibwe surveyor and the Major quickly formed a friendship based on mutual trust and respect. He was one of a select few who shared the Major's dinner table. His association with the Quimby family brought him excellent reading and speaking skills. He thoroughly studied most of the books in the Major's home library. He'd also gained social skills exceeding those of most others on the post.

The chief came to the Sault a solitary traveler. Years earlier, when he lived near the shores of Lake Owasco in the State of New York, he fought bravely alongside the Americans against the British in the war of 1812. Like his father, he was chosen by his people to be their leader, the ogimaa, the chief.

But smallpox, that dreadful gift from the white man, claimed too many of his people, including his wife and sons, and brought too many tears. The chief needed to journey from this place. His travels took him far from his first home, far from the pain. Keeping memories of his loved ones close to his heart, he moved farther and farther from his former home to Sault Ste. Marie and the friendship of Major Quimby and his family.

The chief was tall, strong, had sparkling eyes, a warm smile, and a warmer heart that led to frequent invitations to share the elders' tobacco. Seeking to learn and to share his knowledge with those he visited, he became known as a trader of wisdom. Each journey, village, and person increased the chief's insight as he traveled from Hudson Bay to Gitchee Gumi, the big lake the whites called "Superior."

The chief was a man of vision, understanding the differences between the Indian's life and the white man's way. He also understood that more and more white men would come to the northern waters just as his people, following another vision many years earlier, traveled beyond Gitchee Gumi. His ancestors sought a new home and a new life. They discovered both in the land called Ouisconsin, a place with many lakes and rivers filled with menoomin, the good grain that grows in water and gives life. The whites called it wild rice.

One evening, after sharing dinner with the Major and his family, the chief's life suddenly changed. Following an enjoyable meal of smoked pork, buttered squash, and flat bread with molasses, he retired to his lodge. Hours later, he had the dream. Perhaps a nightmare, perhaps a vision, he knew Wenebojo, the Anishinabe spirit, presented it to him.

The chief dreamt of a fire. Edora, the daughter he adored, perished in the flames. He was wrongly blamed, put in chains, and sentenced to be hanged.

The chief escaped, in this nightmare, fleeing into the forest, the Major and his soldiers close behind. A life or death clash ended with the chief looking down on his friend, a knife sunk deep in the Major's chest.

Wenebojo then woke the chief, who now lay in a cold sweat, his heart pounding in the dark.

As in many dreams, he saw no reason, no rhyme. Making no sense of it, he drifted back into his troubled sleep. Wenebojo brought him a second vision—two shining stars in a sparkling sky, the chief there with them. Wenebojo whispered, "Thirteen days you must travel westward along the southern shores of Gitchee Gumi. Only there will you find your peace—only there."

The chief rose from his uneasy sleep, knowing what he must do. Well before dawn, with no one else about, he gathered his few belongings, took them down to his canoe, and silently paddled west. He would seek out the two stars. There would be no fire at the post. The vision had been broken. The horrible events foretold now dissolved, vanishing like northern lights chased by the early morning sun. The chief would never again see the Quimby family or the land he came to think of as his home.

Each silent stroke of the chief's paddle left small whirlpools of cold, Gitchee Gumi water spinning behind. As his canoe glided swiftly along the shore, two eagles watched from the top of a tall white pine. "Is that you, Wenebojo?" he asked the eagles. An otter followed him, diving and surfacing, again and again, curious about this rare sight of man and canoe. "You, Otter," he whispered. "You follow me and watch me. Surely, you are Wenebojo in disguise."

A doe and two fawns watched him from the shore, motionless. "You don't fool me, Wenebojo. You are keeping your eyes on me, waiting to play your tricks."

Stroke after stroke, the chief moved away from Sault Ste. Marie and closer to his new life, new home, and many new friends, each with stories of their own.

The mystery of what lie ahead began to unfold. Across the land of the northern lakes, the *Treasure of Namakagon* would soon become legend.

(Author's note: Chief Namakagon was a real person and, although THE TREASURE OF NAMAKAGON is fiction, it is based closely on the history of 19th century life in northwestern Wisconsin. The story told in this chapter is based on Chief Namakagon's interview with a Chicago newspaper reporter in 1882.)

The Cabby

There he lingered
In the rain,
Hunched from pain, deep within.
Pain from sin. Pain from dread.
“Not my choice,” he said.

There she lay
In rain so cold.
It washed her blood ’cross cobblestone
And from the dress her mother’d sewn
Only days before.

“’Twas not my’ choice!”
No one heard.
“Not my will to kill again.
Not my desire, nor my wish.”
Words all lost within the mist.

His knife as keen
As any found
In Boston’s crumbling shanty town
Now lay before him on the ground,
Near the corpse so still.

He shouted out,

"Not my will!"

Still the fog absorbed each word.

Still the night concealed him there,

Waiting for another fare.

The Bones of Ole Johnson

Far up the old Wisconsin
Lie the bones of Ole Johnson.
His ghost it swims the river night and day.
Ole's looking for a tool
That he dropped in a deep pool.
When the log jam he was fightin' did give way.

The dynamite they used
Was not correctly fused
And blew the pine high above the bay.
As for Ole Johnson's crew,
Across the logs they flew!
But Ole lost his footing on the way.

His men their god did thank
When they made the river bank.
But Ole dropped his Peavey in the drink.
He dove into the pool,
This timber-drivin' fool,
Before he even had the time to think.

Up Ole came for air
But only logs were there,
A-turnin' in the churning icy foam.
Far from the river's shore,
He cursed the logs and swore
That he'd bring that Peavey back or ne'er come home.

Pine floating overhead,
Ole swam the river bed,
He hoped to bring his precious Peavey back.
And, above the river's noise,
Shout, "Found it!" to his boys.
The mark of any worthy lumberjack.

His men all stood and stared
Their concern for Ole shared,
Watching all the thrashing, bashing pine.
While below, Ole did swim,
The chance now growing slim
That they'd see poor Ole Johnson down the line.

A thousand pounds each log did weigh,
Or even more, I would say.
Half-a-million floatin' to the mill.
Ole Johnson down below,
A-countin' as they go,
And the ghost of Ole Johnson counts them still.

Now, if you take a float
In a kayak, tube, or boat,
On a Wisconsin crick or creek or river, too,
And you feel a sudden bump
Or you hear a muffled thump,
Know that the ghost of Ole Johnson counted you.

And if a Peavey you should see
Below a river flowing free,
Know that Ole left it on the river bed.
Leave it there for Heaven's sake,
Or Ole's place you'll surely take,
Just a-countin' boats a-floatin' over head.

Far up the old Wisconsin,

Lie the bones of Ole Johnson,

A-countin' all the boats as they go through.

If you feel a sudden bump

Or hear a muffled thump,

Know that the ghost of Ole Johnson counted you.

Now my tale of Ole Johnson is all through.

Earwigs

Earwigs cause unbearable pain.
Their gnawing can drive you insane.
Now, don't hoot or holler,
But the one on your collar
Is headed for your tender brain.

Another Mess for Ma to Clean Up

"I'll be damned if I'm gonna tell you where that money is!"

He shoved the barrel of the forty-five into my ribs. "Listen, Frank. You get me that cash or I swear I'll kill you right here, right now! I got nothin' to lose."

"All right. All right. I'll take you to it, dirtball. I don't keep it here. To risky."

We had worked together on a job or two. About three months earlier, he shot a cop and disappeared. I thought he was dead. Would have better all the way around. He was one of those social misfits that prey on anyone weaker than him. A liar, a cheat, a thief. A real hemorrhoid on the anus of life, his girl used to say. That was after she left him. Yeah, the world would have been better off with him dead, all right. No such luck.

Ten minutes later we were three miles east of the city, headed for Eddie McDougal's Riverside Motel and Bar. I flipped Eddie's mother a silver dollar and told her I needed to check into my usual room. Usual, I say, because I used it often. It was at the far end—the seventh in this seven room motel. And it was the only room that had a view of both the highway and the alley.

I had used it often. Every trip from Chicago, in fact. Even though home brew or moonshine was made by nearly every farm in northwestern Wisconsin, it was still illegal to run booze to the speaks, resorts, and taverns. That's what I did. I was a bootlegger.

"Sure thing," said Ma McDougal. "Make dang sure it's clean, this time or I'll have to charge you extra again, Frank. You left me one hell of a mess to clean up last week. I don't like cleaning up after nobody, see?"

I turned the key. The room was small, but all I needed for an overnight stay or a little fun with some lush picked up along the way. There were plenty in the taverns around here. I knew most of them.

"So, where's the money?" said the dirtball.

"For chrisake! Give me a damn chance, will you?" I snapped back. "You think I'd leave it laying out in the open for Eddie to nab?

He shut the door. The motel room was dingy, dark, depressing. A bed, a dresser with a mirror, a four-by-four bathroom with a sink, a stool, but no shower. If you needed a bath, the river was just outside.

"I got no time for this," he said, waving the pistol in my face. "You hand over that money right now or I break both your legs."

I believe he could have and would have. He was as big as he was dumb. And he was plenty dumb. "It's behind the heat register. I'll get it. It'll be worth it just to get you out'a the country and out'a my life—for good this time, right?"

"Git it," he said, thrusting the revolver into my ribs

again.

"Relax, Dirtball. There's no call to get pushy. I'm givin' you the loot, ain't I?

I pulled my jackknife out, flipped it open, using the blade to pull the two screws that held the grill in place. I tossed the grill onto the bed.

"Hand it over," he said, as I pulled the shoebox out of the heat vent. "Come on!"

I flipped open the box. His eyes widened when he saw the stacks of C-notes. He reached for the box. I grabbed the twenty-five auto from under the pile of bills, thrust it into his face and pulled the trigger seven times just as fast as I could.

Now, a Sterling twenty-five auto is not the pistol of choice when time comes to defending yourself. Still, it is a good pal to have on your side in a back ally fight. Today was the first time I had used it. I pulled that trigger seven times, knowing that a twenty-five auto might not stop a big fella like this dirtball with just one shot.

But seven rounds in the face from even a small caliber would be more than anyone could take. Even this big goon. He dropped to the floor, squealing from the pain, his hands covering his face. I wiped the gun clean and tossed it behind the bed as he lay, wiggling and squirming and flopping like some carp out of water.

I didn't care. This was his doing. I grabbed the shoebox and stepped into the bright, early afternoon sunlight. Before I reached my car, I heard the shot. There was little pain, the bullet quickly passing through my chest. I slumped, knelt, then dropped. The shoe box hit the ground, Ben Franklins scattering across the ally like leaves in the breeze.

From the ground, I watched Ma pick up my money, her deer rifle still smoking. When she had them all stuffed back into the shoe box, she stood over me, pointed the muzzle at my head and said, “Looks like you left me another goddamn mess to clean up, Frank. I told you not to, you know. I don’t like cleanin’ up after nobody.”

Death by Ecstasy

"A cup of tea?" She smiled just so.
How could I resist
Her gentle voice and tender eyes?
How was I to know?

Her milky skin, that flowing dress,
How she'd captured me!
Stunned so by her radiance,
How could I ever guess?

Mesmerized, I lost my will.
How did I miss the sign
When the wolf cried in the night,
A howl from distant hill?

Quite tasty was that tea and cream.
How I savored it
And the next she offered me.
How so like a dream.

And dream I did until the end,
An end that came too soon.
Now you, young man, say to me,
How will you defend

Yourself from death by ecstasy?
How might you decline
When a maiden inquires of you,
"Good sir, a cup of tea?"

Heavy Burden

A sorcerer’s most evil curse
Made life for all women much worse.
’Twas really a crime
When he said, “For all time,
You’re bound to lug ’round a big purse.”

The Zombie Apocalypse

Part II: One Month Later

I was in a San Francisco Police Department interrogation room facing a heavy-set cop in a suit that looked like it came straight from the Salvation Army Thrift Store. I had to convince him he had the wrong guy and I had to do it soon.

"Look, Detective," I said, "I am doing post-grad research on what might be the greatest medical discovery of the century. I am close to perfecting a self-replicating, protein-based nano-biotic solution that, when injected into a human vein, will replace normal human function with something far, far better. Instead of living via our bodies' old-fashioned chemical reactions, whereby blood corpuscles carry oxygen and food to the cells, my nano-bot-laced solution will do that. A person on his death bed will instantly have a new life support system—a system we will be able to monitor, adjust, and manipulate with ease. Detective, I am talking about super-high technology coursing through your bloodstream, extending your life for decades—who knows—maybe centuries! I am not the bad guy, here! I am the hero. Get it? I don't know why you're harassing me. You should be out there looking for those damn druggies who broke in and stole my solution!"

"Don't give me that mad scientist crap, kid. I wasn't born last week. You got yourself a meth lab and you and I both know it. You're in trouble, kid. Meth is bad stuff and you're in deep trouble. Deep, *deep* trouble."

"No! You don't understand! I am a scientist. I'm not some druggy. I don't know who stole my solution. All I know is my formula is a perfectly legal, uncontrolled substance and I want it back. All of it. It is mine and it is worth millions to me, billions to the University of California, and possibly trillions to the US economy. You, Detective, need to recover it. You have to get the whole SFPD out there to find it *now*."

"So, kid, if what you say is right, if you *are* doing real research and this stuff is legit—and I'm not saying it is, mind you—then why did those druggies bother stealing it? Makes no sense, kid. What does make sense is that you're handing me a line of bull, that's what. You're working a meth lab and trying to squirm your way out of it, that's what I think."

"No. You're wrong. Now listen closely, Detective. I will speak slowly so you can understand. My lab was broken into last night. I did not do anything wrong. I repeat, Detective, I-am-the-victim, here. Some thieves stole my solution. Just like you, those morons probably thought it was meth. It's not. You need to find them before ... well …"

"Before what, kid?"

"Before they start injecting themselves and others. Before they have a chance to sell it. I had four liters—four *different* liters of solution. They were all very similar in formula, but each flask was slightly different from the others. I was experimenting with some minor variations. Detective, I have run the computer models on these variations and I am certain, upon intravenous injection, these solutions will immediately alter the subject's basic life systems including the nervous system. My earlier formula worked only on expired subjects. This one's improved. It works on live subjects as well as exanimate specimens."

"Layman's terms, kid."

"Sure. Once injected, the subject will see a temperature drop of nineteen degrees. Metabolism will become far more efficient, triggering increased appetite. My nano-bots will bring more food and oxygen to the muscle tissue than normal blood cells ever could, making the subject far stronger. I also know, based on previous experiments, the subject will crave meat protein. Nerve tolerance will escalate, making the subject almost impervious to pain. You might say my solution will turn the subject into sort-of a super being. What the computer models don't show is how my formula variations will affect higher brain function, you know—rational thought."

"You mean ..."

"I mean I don't know, Detective. My research has not reached that stage. The subject may have irregular brain function. No ability to understand basic concepts such as good and bad, right and wrong. Combine that with an excessive craving for meat protein and, well ..."

"Well, what!"

"Detective, there's been a problem or two in the past. Some of the lab animals have turned cannibalistic."

“I don’t care about lab animals.”

“Maybe you should, Detective. You remember that case where the two longshoremen were dismembered down by Pier 7 last month?”

“What of it?”

“Well, was there anything about that case that ... that didn’t get reported to the press?”

“Like what?”

“Like ... was all the *flesh* there? Were there teeth marks on the bones? Did some of the flesh appear to be … eaten, maybe?”

“Okay, kid. Just how do you know about that? What are you are hiding? You have something to do with that case?”

“Me? No. Nothing. Nothing. I was just going to say ...”

“What were you going to say, kid?”

“Look, Detective. You’re wasting time. There is enough for over a thousand doses of my solution floating around out there somewhere. You have to find it—all of it—before you have every meth head in the Bay Area turned into ...”

“What, kid? Turned into what?”

“I’m not saying any more.”

“Turned into what? What!”

“I want a lawyer.”

“Turned into what, kid? *Turned into what!”*

You have now entered

DARKER

Thief of Dreams III

Clearly, reader, you are not faint of heart.
You trod ahead,
With neither fear nor dread
Of what might be found
Down ’round the road’s next bend.
And to that end,
I offer yet another warning.
Scorn not my words, dear friend,
For, should you turn the page again,
Into darker nightmares we descend.

Nevermore

One moonlit night in late December,
How well that night I yet remember,
Shadows cast from dying ember,
Splashed across the floor.

Poe's darkest volumes I did ponder,
And let my mind within them wander.
That's when I found I had grown fond for
His lover, fair Lenore.

When sweet Lenore my heart did take.
Soon, like Poe, my heart did break.
It deeply ached, make no mistake.
How I adored Lenore!

"Fool," said I, "this adoration,
Driven by imagination,
Cannot result in sweet elation."
Yet, I craved her all the more.

"Fool!" I shouted to the rafter,
"Lenore long passed to the hereafter."
Echos fell resembling laughter,
Fell to my chamber floor.

'Twas then Poe's Raven came a-calling
A call that sent my skin to crawling.
A call that struck me so appalling,
Beyond my chamber door.

Before the door latch I could grab,
Inside it flew into my cabin.
Seemingly, keen knives did stab
Into my heart, I swore.

"Fiend," said I, "What are you after,
Perched there, far up o'er my rafter,
Perched there in the chilly draft?
Where hail thee? From what shore?

"Sail thee from some unknown quarters
Thick with Devil's dark supporters?
Be ye Satan's soul transporter?
Say thee, I implore!

"Why linger you? What's your intention?
Why this sudden intervention?
Why curse me with such apprehension,
Bird upon my door?

"Mention now, if you are willing.
This tension my poor heart is killing
With suspense! What word so chilling
Wish ye to explore?

"Speak ye now, foul bird so near.
Say that word I do so fear
You came to share with me in here.
Say thee, 'Nevermore.'"

This evil raptor at me stared.
With burning eyes at me it glared.
But "nevermore" was never shared.
My fear grew ever more.

"Tell me now, why wait you there?
What is this reason you won't share
With me a word? Demon! Declare!
Remark thee, 'Nevermore!'"

Still it sat there, darkly glaring.
Still it lingered, through me staring.
Saying nothing. Never sharing
The dark word, “nevermore.”

“Oh, feathered friend, why do you daunt me?
Befriend me now. Don’t haunt me so.
Know that I mean not to taunt thee.
Pray thee, share my cabin floor.”

It seems those words our fence had mended.
My softer voice, its heart befriended
’Tis then the deafening silence ended
From there above my door.

But “nevermore” remained repressed,
This term that had me so obsessed.
Low, from her breast, the bird expressed,
“I am Poe’s love, Lenore.
Now, fear me nevermore.”

Like Magic

"May I have a volunteer from the audience?"

Hands snapped high into the air.

"You, miss. Yes … you. Please, join me on stage. Together we will astonish and thrill the audience with an amazing journey through the black, brackish alleyways of horror—a gaze into the eyes of Death himself."

He took her hand as she stepped on to the stage. From behind the curtain came the device—a black, coffin-like box on wheels. The magician flipped the sides open, revealing nothing odd.

"Miss, if you please?"

She climbed in, a perfect fit for her petite frame. He closed the box, leaving exposed only her head and feet. The snap of the locks echoed in the now-silent auditorium.

"Ladies and gentlemen, observe," he said, pulling a large, gleaming saw from below the crate. "No tricks. No gimmicks. No different than what your butcher uses daily to saw through muscle, sinew, and bone. I am about to do the same."

With flair and a flip of his black, flowing robe, he spun on his heel, stepping behind the coffin. "And now, I fear, a murderous thing I do. So, say adieu to our fair miss."

He started the cut. Back and forth, back and forth, back and forth. Staring at the audience, she screamed and thrashed and screamed again, blood flowing below. As the show bill in the foyer had proclaimed, her performance that night proved to be the thrill of a lifetime. Back and forth went the gore-laden saw—back and forth, back and forth, back and forth, back and forth.

The audience sounded their delight. Perhaps this show would be worth the price of admission after all.

It was in the morning paper. A magician was found behind the old theater, bound and gagged. His costume, it seems, had been used in a ploy to seek retribution. The daughter of the vengeful imposter's former business partner was the victim.

The police were baffled. The killer had vanished—like magic.

Thief of Dreams IV

You've survived the storm-swept sea this far, and so,
Before the old man stirs,
You need to know
These dark visions will never really end.
Nor pain and grief, my friend,
Until all demons share with you their woe.
Our boat rocks to and fro.
As northward we now go.

The Ballad of the Ne'er Do Well Boys

Far up in the pin'ry they tell of a night
When ten hearty lumberjacks got in a fight.
Gather 'round people. My story I'll tell
Of the boys from the lumber camp called Ne'er Do Well.

In the back room of the Sawmill Saloon
Sat Rusty O'Hara a-whistlin' a tune,
Sharin' a whisky and raisin' some hell
With the boys from the lumber camp called Ne'er Do Well.

Now the Ne'er Do Well boys were a rough-tumble bunch
Who drank, cussed, and gambled and, I've got a hunch
Would stand close beside, if you needed them there
But showed you no mercy if your dealin' warn't square.

Now a fella named John Bob, he pulled up a stool
And tossed in his ante, this Norwegian fool.
The Ne'er Do Well boys, their eyes couldn't believe
When he dealt from the bottom with cards up his sleeve.

Rusty O'Hara was first man to speak.
He said, "Johnny Bob, now, we weren't born last week.
We see that you're fixin' to swindle away
From Ne'er Do Well lumberjacks their hard-earned pay."

"Them's fightin' words, mister," ol' John Bob did shout.
That's when our boy Rusty punched him in the snout.
Out onto the street these big brawlers did go,
A-punchin' and a-fightin' in two feet of snow.

By a boot John got waffled, right square on the chin.
He spit out two teeth, then stood with a grin.
You'll have to do better, you Ne'er Do Well men.
I ain't bound to let you knock me down again.

They fought and they floundered with snow underneath.
John Bob lost an ear lobe to Ole's old teeth.
Swede, Pete, and Elmer next got in their licks.
Them Ne'er Do Well boys they don't put up with tricks.

They wrestled and battled up and down the street.
But John Bob kept gettin' back up on his feet.
They fought all that night long and into the day,
When Rusty said, "Boys, I got something to say."

"Any man willin' to fight through the night
'Gainst ten other men, right through to daylight,
Is certainly worthy of respect from me
And the Ne'er Do Well boys in the big pinery."

"So if you quit swindlin' and cheatin' at cards,
We'll share us a whisky and all become pards.
Oh, John Bob, you're all right so come sit a spell
With the boys from the lumber camp called Ne'er Do Well.

Now, in the back room of the Sawmill Saloon
Sits John Bob a-tryin to whistle a tune,
Sharin' a whisky and raisin' some hell
With his newly found friends from the camp, Ne'er Do Well.

Namakagon and the Great Makwaa

(Excerpt from Chapter 8 of THE TREASURE OF NAMAKAGON
© 2012 James A. Brakken, BadgerValley.com)

A coal-black raven flew above the hunter and his prey, calling out an alarm. The huge bear, this great makwaa, did not heed the bird's warning.

Namakagon's blood pounded in his ears as the bear, much larger than he had previously thought, came closer and closer. A slight breeze on his face assured him the bear would not catch his scent. But it did catch the smell of the venison suet he had set for bait. The bear looked in every direction, but poor eyesight prevented it from seeing the motionless hunter who knelt behind the balsam blind a short distance away.

Chief Namakagon's bow was now fully drawn. When the bear reached the point directly below the suet, it stopped. The hunter's heart was pounding harder and harder now, but he could not shoot. The angle was wrong. He might only wound the great animal if the arrow hit the bony shoulder rather than entering the chest. He waited in silence at full draw, arms trembling.

The bear sniffed the air, looked up, and saw the suet above him. He stood on his hind legs, his belly and great black chest facing the chief, not ten steps away. The hunter put more tension on the bowstring, took final aim, then relaxed the fingers of his strong right hand.

Just as the enormous bear plucked the tallow from the branch, the arrow flashed through the crisp, morning air.

Namakagon's eyes opened wide as he watched the giant makwaa charge straight at him. The bow fell from his hand as he reached for his knife but, before he could pull it, the great bear crashed through his balsam blind and bounded across, smashing him to the ground below its huge front paws.

(Author's note: Although fiction, this excerpt from Chapter 8 of THE TREASURE OF NAMAKAGON is based on a true-life experience.)

Are you next?

A troll's friendship is so hard to earn.
His visitors often do learn
The bones scattered there
Around the troll's lair,
Are guests who will never return.

G. Doré
BERTRAND. Sc.

Oh, Shanty Boy

Oh, shanty boy,
You don't know how I fear for thee,
Out in the cold
And snowy pinery.
From dawn to dark
You risk your very life for me.
I pledge to you,
Your love I'll always be.

Beyond farm fields
Wisconsin's pines they called to you.
All winter long
You slave your life away
To keep our farm
From banker's hands. That's all you do.
Dollar-a-day is what the bosses pay.

Majestic pines,
They stretch almost to heaven's door.
When they descend, run far beyond the crown.
For, should you fall,
Your handsome face I'll see no more.
They seek revenge on those who cut them down.

Oh, shanty boy,
You don't know how I fear for thee
Out in the cold
And snowy pinery.
From dawn to dark
You risk your very life for me.
Oh, shanty boy, I pledge your love I'll always be.

Now what's this news?
You ne'er returned to shanty door.
A falling pine
Seems was the death of thee.
And now I learn
The comp'ny boss had pushed for more.
And a widowmaker stole my man from me.

So here we are,
Your son and wife now wearing black.
Awaiting you
But no more to embrace.
The lumber train
Will bring you down the railroad track.
One more man the comp'ny must replace.

Oh, shanty boy,
I weep for thee. I weep for thee,
Out in the cold
And snowy pinery.
It breaks my heart
You gave the pine your life for me.
Oh, shanty boy, I pledge your love I'll always be.

The boss man says
You failed to work the winter through.
And now I learn, we shall not get your pay.
The bank's foreclosed.
Now leave this farm is what we'll do.
No coin in hand and nowhere else to stay.

And so we, too
Will venture to the pinery.
A sporting house
Is where I'll earn my keep.
And your sweet son
Will soon become a shanty boy,
While in the dreary graveyard you do sleep.

Oh, shanty boy,

I weep for thee. I weep for thee,

Out in the cold

And snowy pinery.

It breaks my heart,

You gave the pine your life for me.

I pledge to you,

Your love I'll ever be.

Oh, shanty boy, know that your love I'll always be.

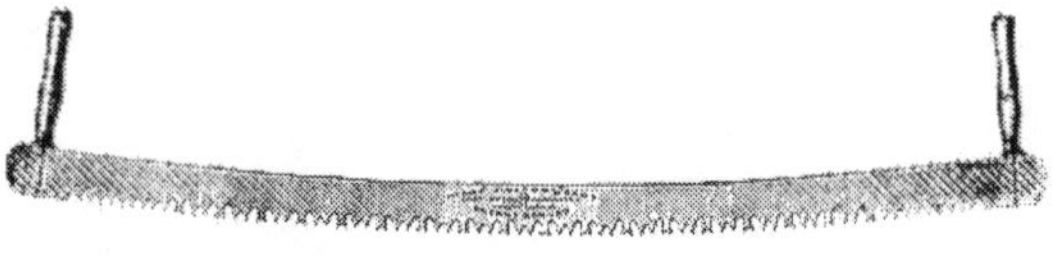

That's One

From their wedding they did ride,
A logger and his bride,
Dreaming of a life of wedded bliss.
The buggy that they rode,
Soon stopped along the road.
The mare, it seems, felt something was amiss.

"That's one!" the man exclaimed.
Tugging on the reins,
The buggy soon resumed its bumpy ride.
The mare did clip and clop
But then again did stop
Munching on some tender leaves 'longside.

"That's two," the logger screeched,
As for his whip he reached.
And, on the buggy flew as he cursed.
But as the sun got hot,
The horse soon slowed her trot
Stopping at a stream to quench her thirst.

He shouted "Horse, that's three!
Now you've angered me,
Testing me for third and final time."
With a bullet to the head,
He shot the poor mare dead.
To his young bride this seemed an awful crime.

"Why, that, my husband, dear,
Was clearly very near
The dumbest thing any man has done!
You shot our only horse!
We're stranded here, of course."
That's when the logger turned and said, "My dear, that's one!"

Beneath the Clay

I quarreled with my love one day.
What set us off, I cannot say.
And now she lays in Central Park,
Her cold and moldy grave so dark.
And there she'll stay,
Beneath the clay,
Forever and a day.

She's not alone, this child so fair,
My other loves are also there.
Each one dear to my heart yet,
Oh, their fate so early met.
Oh, how I do so regret
How they must stay
Beneath that clay,
Forever and a day.

Another love I soon did charm,
Another child, so soft and warm.
This one I pledged would see no harm.
I swore to her I would be loyal.
Never ending blissful joy'll
Be hers and mine, this princess royal.
She'll never lay
Beneath that clay
Forever and a day.

I cherished her, this child so dear.
Ev'ry night I held her near,
Until another day'd begun,
Until we saw the rising sun.
How could she know what I had done?
Had she been told, this fair one?
My crimes were known to only one
And those who lay
Beneath that clay
Forever and a day.

My murd'rous, evil past, it seems
Did come to her between dark dreams.
Streaming in came ghoulish screams,
Visions clear as moonlight beams.
My other loves did beg that she,
Even the score and set them free.
Poison was the tool she chose,
A clever choice, I suppose.
Now 'tis I who lay
Beneath this clay
Forever and a day.

The Widowmaker

(Excerpts from Chapters 22 & 23 of THE TREASURE OF NAMAKAGON
© 2012 James A. Brakken & BadgerValley.com)

Tor and his ox team were eight miles from his pa's camp when the sun came out and the wind shifted. Now a warm, south breeze combined with the sun's rays to melt the snow. Tor's ox team dragged a three hundred pound v-shaped plow made from oak timbers. When he reached the timber landing at the end of the trail, sixteen-year-old Tor turned the oxen homeward. His return trip was faster, a pleasant ride through the snowy woods on this sunny, mid-December day in 1883.

Near the camp, Tor met up with one of the saw teams. The two sawyers felled a big pine that missed its mark and now leaned into another tree. The top of this leaning tree was hung up in a tangle of limbs and branches. The cutting crew's attempts to free it were not working. They chained the butt of the log to their horse team but the horses could not budge the giant white pine.

"Looks like you got a good ol' widowmaker, fellas," called out Tor. "You're welcome to use my ox team if need be."

The swamper threw a chain over the oak plow pulled by Tor's team and hooked the other end onto the stubborn tree. Tor and the teamster slowly coaxed the beasts forward. The five-foot-diameter butt of the tree began to move, then stopped again. They urged the oxen and the horses ahead once more. The animals strained, digging their calked, iron shoes into the frozen, snowy turf beneath and placing enormous strain on the chains.

High above them came a deafening *ca—rack!* A large limb sixty feet up in the other tree snapped violently and the gigantic pine plummeted toward the earth. As it fell, the thirty-foot broken limb sprung through the air and fell not three feet from Tor, missing his oxen but striking the horse beside him.

The huge workhorse reared up, snapping the harness. Both horses, crying out in fear, fell to the ground, hooves flailing as the tree slammed to the ground nearby. The oxen lurched forward. Both Tor and the teamster dove away from the animals, covering their heads. In seconds, the accident was over and the horses and men getting back up.

"You fellas all right?" shouted the teamster. "Anybody hurt?"

"I'm fit," called out one of the sawyers.

"Me, too," piped in the swamper.

"I'm all right," yelled Tor. One man did not answer.

"Where's Mason?" shouted the teamster. "*Mason!*"

"Here—over here," called out the second sawyer.

Mason Fitch lay in the snow face up. A three-foot-long splinter, part of a larger pine branch, stuck out of his thigh. Tor and the other teamster plowed their way through the deep snow to the fallen man. Mason groaned as Tor slowly lifted his leg to find the splinter went all the way through. The swamper brought over his double-bit ax, and with a swift swing, separated the splinter from the branch. The injured lumberjack screamed in pain. Bleeding badly, he began slipping into shock.

"Tourniquet!" shouted teamster Henry Tilden. Immediately the swamper ran to the horse team. Using his razor-sharp ax as a knife, he cut a six-foot length of rawhide strap from the reins. The teamster tied a loop around the leg above the wound, inserted a two-inch thick pine branch and twisted it tightly. The bleeding stopped.

"Where'd you learn that?" asked Tor.

"I worked in a hospital back east during the war," Henry replied. "Virginny. I saw plenty of soldiers with their arms and legs dang-near blowed off from Yankee mini balls. The soldiers who came in with tourniquets usually lived. The poor fellas who didn't have 'em, well, they just bled to death where they fell." He checked over his knot. Looking up at the injured logger he said, "Mason, let's get you back to camp so Sourdough can have a look at you."

"I don't want to lose my leg, Henry Tilden," cried Mason. "I ain't gonna spend the rest of my years with a dang stump fer a leg. Promise me, Henry. Promise me that you will not let Sourdough take my leg!"

"Calm down, Mason. You ain't got such a bad leg here, just a good ol' pine sticker through it. Ol' Sourdough ain't gettin' no soup bone off you this time 'round." No siree. You'll be dancin' Irish jigs by Christmas Day, Fitch."

Mason Fitch lay on a table in the cook shanty, a thick, pine splinter protruding from both sides of his left thigh. Once again the head cook was drafted to patch up a lumberjack after a logging accident. Interrupted while butchering a hog, this appointed doctor wiped his hands on his apron before sliding his butcher knife up Mason's pant leg, slitting it to the crotch. He cut through the man's long johns, wet with melted snow and blood, and pulled back the layer of red wool.

"Best loosen that tourniquet for a time, Henry," he said.

"Don't take my leg, Sourdough," begged the pale, weak lumberjack.

Sourdough peered at him over his round, wire-rimmed glasses. "Don't you worry now, Mason. Your leg will be good as new in no time." He stepped away for a moment, returning with a quart bottle of yellow liquid and a tin cup. He filled the cup and, with help from the others, pulled the wounded worker up to a half-sitting position. "Drink this."

Mason Fitch obeyed, choking down the medicine. "Dear God in Heaven! Sourdough, you tryin' to poison me? What in tarnation was that?"

"Lemon extract," replied the cook, pouring another half-cup. "Here you go, Fitch. Have another."

Mason choked down the second drink. "Why you fillin' me up with lemons, Sourdough? Ain't I suffered enough?"

"Stop your gol-dang complainin', Fitch. There's more spirits than lemons in this stuff. Most shanty boys in camp would give a half-day's pay for a pull on this bottle. Stronger than that rotgut whisky they serve in town. Mason, I confess that I take a nip myself now and then—just to clear my sinuses, you understand."

After a third drink, the men helped Mason lay down again.

"Hank, Will, Tor, you fellas hold him tight now. Mason, we're gonna pull out that there splinter. It's bound to hurt some so bite down on this rag," he said, plugging a dishrag in the man's mouth. "Now grab the edges of the table and hold on, boy."

Mason did. With a quick jerk, the head cook yanked out the long, blood-soaked, pine splinter. Mason bit down hard and did not utter a sound.

"Good, good," said Sourdough. "Henry, grab that empty sauce pan off the counter and fill 'er up with snow. Tor, hand me my sewing kit—that green box on the shelf over the sink." Henry and Tor complied. Sourdough took a handful of snow, packed it into a ball and placed it on the open wound.

"Henry, you hold this tight for a minute. Push hard," he ordered. The amateur doctor then pawed through the green box until he found a large, curved sewing needle. He pulled three feet of cotton thread from a wooden spool and snipped it off with a small scissors. Tipping his head back and squinting through his glasses, he threaded the needle. The backwoods surgeon removed the bloodied snow, pitching it across the room, straight into the slop bucket.

"All right, Fitch," said Sourdough. "I am gonna stitch up this side, first. Might pinch a bit." He poked the needle through Mason's chilled hide. The others watched as the camp cook sewed the wound closed, tying each stitch securely. Mason grimaced with each push and pull on the needle.

"Thirteen stitches, Mason," said Tor. "Not so lucky."

"Lucky?" said Sourdough. "I'll tell you about luck. Mason, if you had been standin' a bit to the left, you'd be soon singin' in the Vienna Boys Choir. That's how lucky you are, boy." Then, to his assistants, "All right, turn him face down so we can stitch up the other side."

With help from his co-workers, Mason Fitch rolled over clumsily, now with a grin on his face. "I think the lemons are wearin' off, Sourdough. How about another swig?"

"Nope. No more for you. Your damage ain't bad enough to warrant me givin' up any more of my bottled goods. Next time you taste my lemon extract will be in one of my Christmas pies."

"Don't make my leg look too ugly, Doc."

"Mason, I'll make it look so gol-dang pretty that every sportin' gal in town will pay a dollar just to steal a peek at my fancy needlework. Fitch, you'll make more a night than they do."

Beastly Feastings

"Trolls are such a bother!"
My father shouted out.
"They've routed out my garden, row by row.
Our hens no longer lay.
Our cow has run away.
There's only one solution that I know.

The ogre I will summon.
From yonder hill he'll come
And kill those pesky trolls, one by one.
And when he's done, we'll nay
See those trolls another day.
He'll roast them in his oven till well-done.

Or, for his sausage, grind them.
No more, 'round here, we'll find them.
Trollish Polish sausage, his delight!
Their feet this beast will pickle.
His tongue those trolls will tickle.
They'll all, by nightfall, be well out of sight.

Oh, how this beastly ogre
Will feast upon those trolls.
He'll roll their eyeballs in his sugar bowl.
Their entrails he will take,
Making innards into cake,
And, from troll belly, bake a jelly roll.

The brisket he will broil,
Braise, or boil in oil.
With wine he'll dine by shining candlelight.
When finished with his deed,
A midnight snack he'll need.
He'll suck their salty bones in soft starlight."

"But tell me, Daddy dear,"
This laddie cried, in fear,
"When trolls have died, what will the ogre eat?"
My father slowly said,
"When all the trolls are dead,
Children are his favorite beastly treat."

Gramma's Noggin

Gramma bumped her noggin
Up on the Namekagon
While floatin' down the river in a boat.
She noticed not the tree
The beaver cut, you see
It rang her bell with quite an awful note.

A thousand trees or more,
She passed along the shore.
Who knew this one would bean her on the head?
Just before it fell,
A beaver gnawed it well.
An evil twist of fate it must be said.

Or was it Grampa's little shove
That brought the tree from up above?
No one will know what caused the final curtain.
'Cept Grampa and the beaver
And the judge. He's a believer
Less in fate and more in facts he finds quite certain.

Gramma bumped her noggin
On the River Namekagon.
Now Grampa's in the jailhouse feelin' sad.
The judge went with the facts
When the sheriff found Grampa's ax.
As for the beaver, he had nothing more to add.

That beaver's out there yet,
Chewing briskly, you can bet.
Soon a falling tree will splash again.
So, when on the Namekagon,
Be sure to guard your noggin
And think of dear old Grampa in the pen.

Bloks Bergs
Verrichtung.

Three Dragons

The Second Dragon

Lit torch in my left hand and sword in the right, I ventured deeper into the dragon's damp, dark cave. An abrupt crunch of bone underfoot told me I had found one of the missing brave suitors of the Princess of Fairland by the Sea. Lowering my torch, I discovered the bones picked clean. The larger of the teeth marks were distinctly those of a dragon, the smaller those of rats. Mingled there with the bony evidence were greenish-brown scales—dragon scales shed as a shepherd's dog sheds hair. Scale and bone crunched under my weight as I crept deeper into the darkness.

"Who dares trespass?" said a second gravelly voice. "Who!"

"'Tis I, a messenger with sad news I so regret to announce."

"And what is this sad news you bring?" said the beast.

"I fear your dear fellow dragon no longer inhabits these quarters, sir."

"What say ye? No longer here? And what, pray tell, is the reason for his absence?"

"He is dead, Sir Dragon."

"Dead?"

"Dead as dead can be."

"Bah! How do I know you speak the truth, messenger?"

"Look here," I said, tossing the severed dragon head high in the air.

As the second beast stretched out his neck to catch in his teeth the head of the first, my sword flashed through the air and two severed dragon heads plopped onto the filthy floor of the cave. The creature's great body collapsed, wriggling, twisting, and, from its decapitated carcass, discharging gore before me until, ankle-deep in blood, bile and spew, I stared down at a motionless mass of malodorous, dead dragon. The rotten stench emanated by the vile creature was nearly more than I could endure. I hurriedly lashed both dragon heads to my now-sagging belt, confident now that dragons were, indeed, not invincible. In fact, they almost seemed easy prey for man with sword intent on winning the hand of a princess and the lands of her majestic father. Two dragons dead, one dragon left to kill, I pressed deeper into the musty cave.

Der Apt.

Death's Dreadful Schedule

Death has such a dreadful schedule.
Scouring 'cross the land,
Hourglass in hand,
Waiting 'neath dark willow,
No pillow soft on which his skull might lie.

Death's blade must weigh so heavily.
Quite a load to bear,
Night and day it's there.
Rarely do we see him
Freed from that gruesome, grisly scythe.

Still, Death grins his evil grin.
Though cold wind might blow,
Though the whirling snow
Slows him from his reaping,
Postponing him from sweeping up your soul.

Still, Death keeps on treading,
Adding to his score,
Padding even more
His sad'ning spirit tallies,
Those souls he doth keep adding to his scroll.

D.H.

Welcome to

DARKEST

Thief of Dreams V

Still you linger here, oh Thief of Dreams,
Seeking fear and even darker scenes.
Do turn the pages
And journey through the ages.
Fearing not the shadow just ahead.

Onward tramp now, voyeur that you are.
Camp in the mist and fog upon the moor.
Don't sway. Don't swerve.
Observe now tales even more unnerving
As you peer beyond those now long dead.

Another tale awaits you now, you know.
Turn the page and dim the lamp down low.

Them

Frank Cavanaugh wiped the blood from his neck with his handkerchief before knocking twice on the big, mahogany door. It swung open. He crossed the modestly decorated office, approaching the receptionist. She looked up. “Yes?”

“I … I’m not exactly sure, Ma’am, but I believe you might be … expecting me?”

“You have an appointment?”

“Appointment? Well, not really. No. I mean …”

“We strongly recommend appointments, Sir. Such high traffic nowadays.”

“I’m sorry, Ma’am. I didn’t intend to … actually, I don’t even know why I’m here. Or, for that matter, where I am.”

“I can check the schedule. Mister …”

“Cavanaugh. Frank Cavanaugh.”

“Kavanaugh … Kavanaugh.”

“With a ‘C’, Ma’am.”

“Oh, yes. Here it is. Francis Taylor Cavanaugh. Saint Louis, Missouri, right?”

“Saint Louis? No. Oh, yeah, Saint Louis, but that was long ago. Before Chicago, Milwaukee, Los Angeles.”

“Well, all we can go by is where you were born, Mr. Cavanaugh. We know precisely when and where you were born but, well, you can see the problem with trying to keep track of all the places everyone goes during their stay.”

“Their stay?”

“In life. You know, where they go while living here—here on Earth. Planet Earth?”

“No. I guess I don’t know. What, exactly, do you mean?”

“Oh. Okay. You’re one of those. You must have just passed. You haven’t been advised yet.”

“Advised? Advised of what? And what do you mean, passed?”

“All right. It’s not my regular job, but I’ll tell you anyway. You lived on Earth for… let’s see… forty-one years, three months, twelve days, seven hours, and almost twenty-nine minutes. Does that sound about right?”

“Well, I suppose. But you make it sound … um, like …”

“Like a final figure? A sum total?” Like you are at the end of your time?

“Yes, that’s it. You make it sound final.”

“Well, that’s what it is, Francis. It’s final. You, Francis, have reached the end of your stay.”

“What? End of my stay? What do you mean by that? And just who are you, anyway?”

“Me? Oh, I’m Marcia. Marcia Gabriel. My family’s been in this business since, well, I don’t know when. We Gabriels help people who are moving. Francis, I really do not like being the one to tell you, but your time here is done. You were driving south on Ventura tonight, right, Francis?”

"It's Frank. I go by Frank. And, yes, I was on Ventura tonight. I always take Ventura home from work.

"Well, Francis … er, Frank, there was an accident. You were killed. You're dead, Frank. You've already been replaced by a newborn. Your time on Earth is over. Done. You can't stay. You're moving on, Frank—moving on to a new location. Pretty exciting, huh?"

"I'm … dead? Dead? Ridiculous! You're crazy! And what the hell do you mean by 'new location'?"

"Frank, in spite of what you may have been led to believe, Earth is only one of an overwhelming number of planets where humans exist. Each location is in need of improvement. Humans have been chosen to make those improvements. Think of it, Frank. Of all the species in the whole, wide Universe, it is humans who have been chosen to do thousands upon thousands of years of work improving things. Imagine! Trillions of humans are out there developing, cultivating, enriching the multitude of planets in each of untold millions of galaxies! Humans, Frank! The Chosen Ones!"

"And who, exactly, are we improving your multitude of planets for, may I ask?"

"Who? Well, the hosts, Frank. Our superiors. Them."

"Them. Them?"

"Yes, you know, them—those in control. Our hosts, Frank. The ones in charge. *Them!*"

"So, okay, Marcia, if I understand correctly, what you are telling me is that I am no longer alive and my entire life was spent improving this place for—for someone else? And I am now going to another planet to spend another lifetime working to improve things there for ...*Them?* Is that what you are saying?"

"Yes, Frank, I suppose that sums it up pretty well."

"And here I thought I was working to improve things for myself, my family, my kids, and grandkids. But, actually, according to you, I was working for somebody or something else."

"Yes, but you make it sound like a bad thing. It's not, Frank. Really! It's not! Yes, it is true we improve things for them. But, along the way, while helping them, we also improve life for all humans. It's a symbiotic relationship, Frank. See?"

"But, in truth, in the final tally, Marcia, we humans are no more than slaves who are working all across the universe to improve things for Them, whoever they are, right?"

"Well, yes, I suppose you could look at it that way."

"Really? That's what life is? That's the final solution to Man's eternal search for the true meaning of life? We're mere servants? Slaves? Really?"

"You could say that, Frank."

"Marcia, if what you're saying is right, then everything Man has done, every decision, every exploration, every invention, hell, every murder, every genocide, every conquest, every—everything has been done because of or on behalf of … Them?"

"Yep, that sizes it up."

"Religion, too, Marcia? You mean to say we humans believe all that we believe—believe in our gods, fight religious wars, pit people against people, all as some kind of unintended consequence of this unseen, obscure scheme to improve the planets? Improve the planets for … Them?"

"'Fraid so, Frank, although that's not really part of the overall plan. It's just what humans do. It's the way humans are. You could call it human nature."

"I'm not buyin' this. You're tellin' me that I have been on this planet, Planet Earth, convinced that I am working to better myself and the lives of my family members, but, in truth, according to you, Marcia, I am just here to improve Planet Earth for some unknown …"

"Not really unknown, Frank. Unknown to most, but definitely not unknown to all."

"What do you mean?"

"Our hosts, Frank. Our hosts. They are not unknown."

"Well, who the hell are they? I want to meet them. I want to meet them right now, Marcia! I've got something to say to them—believe me. Something to say, all right!"

"I'm … I'm afraid they don't understand our language, Frank."

"Don't understand our langua… How can that be? What nationality are they? Surely someone can talk with them."

"Talk all you want, Frank. They won't understand a word."

"Marcia, exactly who are these … these … creatures who don't speak our tongue, who have somehow enslaved humans to improve millions upon millions of planets for them? Tell me, who are these mysterious superiors of ours?"

"Sure you want to know, Frank?"

Francis Taylor Cavanaugh stared coldly into Marcia Gabriel's eyes.

"All right, Frank, all right! But don't say I didn't …"

"Dammit, Marcia! Who are they?"

"I don't know what they're called where you're going, Frank. But here? Here, we call them *Earth*worms."

PUNCH'S ALMANACK FOR 1882.
MAN·IS·BVT·A·WORM·

Vengeful Curse

Her curses we just could not take
So we burned the old witch at the stake.
Now 'tis we who must pay.
We'll die the same way.
For making that heated mistake.

Something in the Shadows

The hangman grins an evil grin.
His sin he does not recognize.
He's not aware he'll be the prize
Of something in the shadows.

This hangman ties a worthy knot
He's practiced many years.
No tears he sheds for those who swing
No comfort nor consideration
For their dark anticipation
Of that sudden snap of rope.

Something in the shadows waits,
Twice, no thrice his size,
Or larger, still, and
Thrilled to see him kill again,
Wanting to collect the prize of yet another soul
To take below, far below, into the depths of Hell.

Our hangman tends his daily task,
Never understanding
These punishments he's handing now
Will be his own reward:
Eternal snap of his own rope.
No hope for his salvation.
You should have known, oh, Hangman,
We reap what we have sown.

And you, dear one, what sow you now?
You know just what I mean.
What awaits when Reaper strikes?
Perhaps, like some, you will find
A kind eternity?
Or the hangman's destiny?
The choice is yours to make.
Make it soon—for Heaven's sake.

Three Dragons

The Third Dragon

Narrow, ancient steps led me down and down and down into a vast, dimly lit, foul-smelling chamber. I crossed the flagstone floor, following a narrow path between piles of dragon excrement, some old, dry, and crusted, others appearing recently deposited. An immense, oaken door, unbarred and somewhat ajar, beckoned me to open it. I pulled it no more than a hand-width when its rusted hinges' faint creaking must have alerted my quarry, who, from the other side, charged the great door, bashing it open, and driving me back into the chamber. Falling rearward, I tripped over a pile of scat, landing flat on my back as the monster descended upon me. My sword was of no avail in such close quarters. Yet, as the great, revolting beast opened his cavernous jaws to sink rot-laden teeth, my dagger stabbed through his great, red eye and penetrated well into his brain. Like the others, bright orange blood spewed forth, drenching me, the flagstone floor, and nearby piles of dragon dung. The hideous creature emitted a wild, bone-chilling screech before reeling back into the door. A loud slam of the stalwart, wooden gateway echoed as the dead dragon slumped and slid down onto the filthy, dung-littered, bloody floor.

My sword made quick work of liberating dragon head from body. Preparing to depart the putrid, dark, foul-smelling cave for the glowing, white castle, I lashed the third grim trophy to the others. My quest was complete. I had all three prizes and felt confident the Princess of Fairland by the Sea and all she would come to inherit would be mine forever. Before taking my leave, though, my curiosity begged me to look beyond that massive door. Pushing the decapitated dragon carcass aside, I swung wide the hefty oaken gate. There, in the dim light, were the bony remains of the other six champions who'd earlier sought the same reward and treasure as I. Squinting now, I tried to make out the nature of other, rather roundish objects scattered hither and yon. I stepped forward, reached, and grasped one, holding it to the soft light drifting in through the doorway behind. It was yet another dragon head. I opened the door even wider now, counting the others there among the bones of my fellows, nineteen, twenty, twenty-one heads of dragons.

"Odd," I said aloud, "that six men lay among twenty one dragon heads and yet another hero lies dead near the cave entrance."

"There's reason for it, murderous intruder," came another gravelly voice from the chamber. I spun around to see not one, but three dragons, each bearing a healthy, albeit hideous head, each freely festooned with fresh scales. "You see, naïve suitor, we simply grow new heads to replace those so often lost in battle."

With that, the largest of the three beasts again slammed the great, oaken door, this time dropping the bar in place, thus dooming me to the grim choice of starvation, consumption of moldy, morbid dragon heads, or falling on my own sword—a sword still dripping with bright orange dragon blood. I cursed the three dragons. My choice was clear.

Dare not Swim in Devil's Lake

These words were carved into a tree
Near water's edge, for all to see:
"Dare not swim in Devil's Lake
Lest Satan steal your soul.
He waits below the surface, calm and still.
He lingers there with eyes ablaze.
What prize does Lucifer desire
To fuel his fire for countless days?
The soul of your existence.

Resistance, friend, will serve you not
When sharpened claws drag you down,
Down into the darkened deep.
'Tis there you'll sleep a fearsome sleep,
A never-ending, fearsome sleep.
Dare not swim in Devil's Lake.
No, dare not swim in Devil's Lake."

I read those words and shed my towel,
Fearing not the Prince of Hell.
Into the lake I dove without a care.
The hand-carved warning taking not,
I made light of words that brought
Fear to all the others standing there.
They watched from shore with horror as
From deep below I felt the claws,
The sharpened claws that pulled me deep
Satan's claws my soul did reap.
'Tis there I sleep my fearsome sleep,
My never-ending, fearsome sleep.

Dare not swim in Devil's Lake.
No, Dare not swim in Devil's Lake.

I—Have—You—Now

(Excerpt from Chapter 33 of THE TREASURE OF NAMAKAGON

Far across town, in a grand Victorian mansion, a single light shone from Phineas Muldoon's third story window. The short, white-haired man sat alone in his library before a large, roll-top desk. On the desk, a kerosene lamp illuminated the map of Lake Namakagon that lay before him. Squinting through the lens of a magnifying glass, he studied the lands surrounding the lake.

The old man placed the glass on the desk and opened a drawer. He picked up a pen, dipped the tip into the inkwell, and drew a circle on the map around the land owned by the Loken family.

"Come spring, Olaf Loken, you and your pitiful Namakagon Timber Company will be at my mercy. You will see what happens when you interfere in my business. And you will learn why I am called *King*. For, you see, Loken, I—have—you—now."

Phineas Muldoon laid his pen on the blotter and capped the inkwell. Pushing his chair back, he stood, staring at the map with a grin. He leaned over his desk, cupped his hand around the glass chimney of the lamp, and, blowing into the chimney, snuffed out the flame.

As the room went black, King Muldoon repeated his words into the darkness. “I have you now, Loken, I—have—you—now.”

The Zombie Apocalypse
Part III, Six Hours Later

SFPD Detectives Terrence Hampton and Logan Quimby watched from their car as the blue BMW pulled into the ally. Both driver and passenger got out. They were young and dressed rather well for San Francisco's Tenderloin District. They stepped between the nearby dumpsters and entered the back door of a three-story brick building on the east side of the alley, about thirty yards from the unmarked squad. Quimby called in the plate number as he and Hampton waited and watched.

Minutes later, the well-dressed men stepped back into the alley, each with a cardboard box. The trunk of the BMW popped open. The boxes went in.

The BMW left the alley and turned west, followed by the unmarked squad car. Both vehicles caught the lights just right and soon the BMW turned onto Fillmore Street. Three blocks later it double-parked in front of Moxie's, one of several clubs in the Fillmore District known to stretch the rules. Detectives Hampton and Quimby passed the BMW and headed north. There was no point in stopping. Too many in this part of town could spot a cop on the prowl. A phone call to an informer would have to take the place of police surveillance. Quimby knew a perp in the neighborhood who needed to stay on the good side of the SFPD. He made the call.

Twenty minutes passed before Quimby's phone rang. The BMW was on the move again. It headed north, then turned west onto Geary Boulevard. Detective Hampton was on its bumper well into the Richmond District when the driver of the BMW pushed his luck on a yellow light. The instant it turned red, Hampton flipped on his siren. The BMW pulled over. Quimby called it in. Hampton stepped out, approaching the driver as the window slowly descended.

"Know what law you broke back there?" he said to the driver.

"You mean the light?"

"What other law do you think I mean?"

"I guess I sorta ran that light, but just a little, Officer."

Quimby, now approached, hand on his weapon, nodding to his partner who spoke again. "I'll need you both to step out of the car, hands where I can see 'em."

"What? Why! What for?"

"Step out now, both of you." Hampton pulled his sidearm from its shoulder holster.

"Okay, okay. Jesus! All I did was push a yellow light. What's the big deal?" he said as he and his passenger stepped out.

“Both of you, hands on the roof! You have any guns on you?” Hampton said as he patted the driver down. Quimby frisked the other man.

“Guns? Of course we don’t have guns! We were in the city for the day and are headed back to Marin County where we live.”

“Any guns in the car?”

“No. No guns, no knives, no bazookas, no army tanks. What the hell is this? We’re businessmen headed home.”

“Any guns in the trunk?”

“Sure, officer. The trunk is full of guns. Stole them from the SFPD armory while you jerks were sleeping! Filled the trunk to the top! Could hardly get the trunk lid closed. What do you take us for, anyway?”

“Hear that, Detective Quimby? I distinctly heard the driver claim to have stolen guns. That’s all we needed to hear,” he said as he popped the trunk lid.

“Officer, there’s nothing in there but a couple of empty boxes. Why don’t you give me my damn ticket and let me get home. I’ll mail a check to your boss tomorrow morning—along with my complaint.”

A second unmarked car pulled in, lights flashing and parking ahead of the BMW. Two black and whites parked behind. Quimby looked in the trunk. “Just the two boxes. Both empty. Looks like that’s it, Terry.”

“What was in those boxes?” Hampton said sternly.

"Just some stuff we dropped off at ... at Goodwill. Or was it St. Vinnies? I don't remember."

"What was in the boxes?"

"None of your business."

"Officer Quimby, call dispatch. Order out a tow truck. Looks like we will have to impound this vehicle, take it apart piece by piece till we find those stolen guns this criminal confessed to."

"Officer, wait. Okay. I picked up a few flasks of some chemical downtown and delivered it to a guy in the Fillmore. I don't know what it was. I was just doing a favor for a friend."

"How many? How many flasks?"

"Four."

"Liters? Four liters?"

"Yes. Liters."

"What was in the flasks?" said Quimby. The other officers now stepped close enough to hear the conversation.

"I'm not sure. Some medicine or something."

"Who'd you deliver them to?"

"Some guy called Dancer. I don't know his real name."

"Must be Willie Dancier. Should've known," said Quimby. "Officers, cuff these guys, read 'em their rights. Get them downtown. Impound the car and have the lab check it out for chemical residue—especially the trunk. Mention nano-bots. That's what the kid called 'em. Nano-bots. We're headed back down to the Fillmore to chase this stuff down."

"Need us there?" asked one of the other officers.

"No. Too many cops will scare Willie off. Quimby and I will handle it. You see what you can learn from these two. Get what you can out of 'em before they wise up and bring in a lawyer. Oh, I think you'll find a pile of cash in their pockets. Impound it as evidence and get it to the lab."

Around eleven-thirty, as Hampton and Quimby watched from their car, a man left Moxie's Club by the back door. As he walked slowly into the light, Quimby saw, on his face, what appeared to be blood. Flashlight in hand, he stepped out to offer help. The man, eyes glazed and seemingly oblivious to Quimby's offer of assistance, turned to walk away.

"Stop. SFPD." said Quimby. The man did not acknowledge the order.

"Stop! Police!" Quimby ordered. There was no reaction from the man. Quimby waved to his partner to pull the car forward.

Hampton started the engine, put the car in drive, and pulled past the man, then turned sharply into his path, cutting him off. The man, having no place to go turned to face the beam of Quimby's flashlight. Confused, he started to climb over the car, then slipped, falling to the ground. He slowly stood, squinted into the flashlight beam, shielding his eyes with his arm. Reaching down, he grabbed the rocker panel of the unmarked squad car and lifted, rolling the car onto its side and pushing it over out of his way. He continued down the alley, ignoring Quimby's repeated orders to stop.

Quimby fired a round into the brick wall ahead of the man. There was no reaction. He leveled his pistol, lowered his aim and fired a round into the man's thigh, hitting the femur, causing him to collapse. Quimby raced the few yards to his partner who was now scrambling out of the open passenger window. As he helped Hampton from the squad car, they heard gasping. They both turned to see the man approaching, leg dragging, with a menacing stare. Quimby raised his weapon and fired two rounds into the man's chest. He reeled from the impact but quickly recovered and continued toward the officers. Quimby fired twice more. The man fell to the pavement, then stood, again approaching the officers when Hampton fired a final round into the assailant's head, dropping him to the ground where he lay motionless.

"My God, Terry! What the hell just happened here?" said Quimby.

"You're askin' me? Logan you call it in. Have 'em send a meat wagon and the county coroner. Tell dispatch to get the chief out of bed, too. He needs to know. Tell them the kid was right. Extreme strength. Impervious to pain. No normal brain function. I'm going in to find Willie Dancier and get that stuff out of his hands before we have more of these brain-dead meth heads to deal with. Call it in, Logan."

Our Lovely Lucy Brown

Milwaukee was a lively place
In thirty-two,
I'm tellin' you.
That's where the mayor first saw her face,
Our lovely Lucy Brown.

She danced naked on the bar.
A south side speak.
Twice a week.
He said with him she would go far.
Our tender Lucy Brown.

Wearing just a feathered hat
She teased him now
And, oh, how
His vulgar mind imagined that
He'd have our Lucy Brown

On his shoulder, she did lean.
And with a grin,
She drank his gin.
They left in his limousine.
Our foolish, Lucy Brown.

They motored to a country inn.
Beyond the glen.
Half past ten.
He parked the car and locked her in.
Too late, oh Lucy Brown.

His mind was bent on having her
And, I trust, so ripe with lust,
He didn't see her hat come down
Our poor girl, Lucy Brown.

He said he would pay her well.
Trade his coins
For her sweet loins.
She told him he could go to Hell.
No trollop, Lucy Brown.

The mayor was set to have his way.
"You'll come around,
Or hike to town.
Now, young lady, walk or lay.
Please me, Lucy Brown."

They found him in his limousine.
Stiff and cold
I've been told.
Her hat pin pierced his heart and spleen.
Oh mercy, Lucy Brown.

Her case was dropped without a trial.
It seems the judge
Held quite a grudge
Against the mayor for quite a while.
A close call, Lucy Brown.

Now she dances as before.
The magistrate
Her steady date.
She wears her hat and nothing more.
Our lovely Lucy Brown.

And as the men all laugh and cheer.
The eight-inch pin
Holds hat ag'in
No masher dares to come too near.
Our lovely Lucy Brown.
Our lovely Lucy Brown.

A Pinery Tale

Johnny Boy, oh, Johnny Boy,
How I love you so.
Johnny Boy, my Johnny Boy,
How was I to know
    You would take a job a'drivin' pine
    Down the old Saint Croix?
    Now I pine, both day and night,
    For my Johnny Boy.

A lumberjack came to me
With news so dark and grim.
He said while rastlin' with the logs,
They sent you for a swim.
    'Tis then they chose to close on you
    Far, too far from shore,
    You sleep, list'ning to the sound,
    Of the river's roar.

Johnny Boy, oh, Johnny Boy
A blackbird you became,
A'drivin' logs down to the mill
In April's pourin' rain.
    Now you lay below the ground
    Oh, my lumberjack,
    In icy water you did drown
    Never to come back.

Twas revenge the spirits sought
For cutting timber down.
The other drivers stood distraught
As Johnny Boy did drown.
    So many boys the river claims
    Each and ev'ry drive.
    We know not many of their names
    Nor who's left to survive.

So many wives and sons remain.
Darling daughters, too.
So many teardrops fall upon
Wisconsin waters, cruel.
    I'll say a prayer to honor you
    And sadly bow my head.
    And send the news on down the line,
    Our Johnny Boy lies dead.

Johnny Boy, oh, Johnny Boy,
How I love you so.
Johnny Boy, my Johnny Boy
How was I to know?

Somewhere in the pinery,
Near the river shore,
You'd lose your life to the pine,
And love me nevermore.

Johnny Boy, oh, Johnny Boy,
You meant so much to me.
I'll come tonight to river's edge,
For with you I must be.

The Curse

Way back a mean witch placed a curse
On women, fair, and, what's worse,
It seems now that she's
Always losing her keys.
They hide deep inside of her purse.

1512

The Kinabalu Affliction

Chicago. Yesterday. I was late after dropping my wife and kids off at the doctor's office. Flashers on, I double-parked my car in a loading zone behind the Congress Hotel and banged on the service door until some guy opened it. Before the hotel worker had a chance to tell me to use the front entrance, I handed him a fifty, told him to watch my car for a few minutes, and stepped onto the service elevator. I rushed into the third floor banquet hall, straight to the lectern. Pulling my notes and reading glasses from the pocket of my lab coat, I looked up to see hundreds of scientists, , and the usual news media teams that always attended the annual science symposium. I simultaneously cleared my throat and adjusted the microphone, then began.

"Ladies, gentlemen, members of the press. As noted in your program, I am Professor Charles Watersteen-Dragg, PhD. I wish to extend my sincere apologies for being late. Unavoidable and, I hope you'll agree in a few moments, understandable.

"Most of you never heard of me—at least not until the recent problem with that family in Haiti. I have been called here to share with you my thoughts about them, this … issue, and what it might mean for the human population.

"Regarding the Haitian family, the preponderance of what I know I learned from network media, as, I assume, have most of you. I learned from CBS that the child, a nine-year-old boy, is now dead. An hour ago, National Public Radio reported that the mother attempted suicide. She is in critical condition. Not expected to survive. The grandmother, who had been living with the family prior to the earthquake, is listed as missing. I believe she died a while ago, perhaps from the same causes as the boy, but that's only my guess. She may have died during the quake and, in spite of the cause, could have been one of many who were simply listed as earthquake victims. As you may know, many deaths were not investigated due to the sheer numbers of dead and injured faced by the Haitian medical community. That leaves the father. He has disappeared. There is a massive search throughout the Caribbean for him as we speak. We need to find him. I believe all of the family members may have suffered the same affliction as the boy.

"Like you, I heard about the horrors this family experienced when the change happened in the boy. I can only imagine the trauma felt by the family. And, as much as I'd like to explain this, er … *phenomenon* to you in concrete terms, I cannot. Besides, that's not why I am here. I can only tell you what I believe caused this based on my earlier research in airborne transmission of microorganisms found in ancient bone samplings and how certain aspects of that research may—I repeat *may*—apply.

"Don't get me wrong, now. I will say again, I do not have the specific answers every scientist, every person in this room desires and deserves. I only have my own limited research and some resulting theories. Furthermore, if those theories are correct, well, as much as I would like to tell you otherwise, I regret admitting we do not have a simple remedy or solution.

“What I can offer, in addition to my aforementioned theories on this, is my knowledge of how rapid an unchecked microorganism of the type found in the bloodstream of the dead boy can travel. Thanks to man’s ingenuity and desire for rapid mobility, modern day aircraft can transport malicious organisms around the world in a day or two. Other transportation innovations, such as automobiles, trains, busses, even bicycles, can aid in the spread. Considering this and the fact that it has been two weeks since the mother died, well, in my opinion, there’s been plenty of time for every person in this room to have been exposed—exposed *multiple* times. The same goes for almost all other humans still on the planet. Only those cosmonauts on the space station Mir and a handful of quarantined patients around the globe might be—*might* be free from the organism, if my research is correct.

“Further, if my theories hold, it is likely that this, ah … *condition*, if you may, could have been here for a good, long time—maybe since the Haitian earthquake of 2010. Some say longer. Maybe five or ten years. We don’t know and won’t know until we see more evidence similar to what happened to the Haitian boy. On one hand, we need to see it soon. On the other, well, it would be best to never see it again. Never.

"There will be those here who doubt my views on this, especially the rampant infectivity via broad-scale, airborne transmission of certain contagions. With all due respect, to those learned individuals, let me say this: over two thousand years ago, a good man gave a sermon on a mount somewhere in the Middle East. The molecules of nitrogen, oxygen, and carbon dioxide that he expelled during that talk have dispersed around the globe over the centuries. They are now in the water of our oceans, in the plants that cover our continents, and, yes, friends, in the very air you and I and every other human breathe. Now, as you may recall from high school physics, atoms that comprise those air molecules cannot, by physical law, be destroyed—at least not by ordinary means. They are recycled again and again and, like it or not, every breath you take contains a few atoms from the same oxygen, nitrogen, and carbon that were breathed in and out by Jesus and every other person who lived long before us. When your Sunday school teacher told you that Jesus was within you, well, that statement was closer to the truth than he or she ever realized. Enough of that.

"Ladies, gentlemen, as I said, I believe we have already been exposed. I also believe there is no known cure, no known antidote, no way for us to fight this microorganism at this time. Not unlike the SARS virus, it attaches itself to exhaled molecules of CO_2 and uses Man's own breath as its dispersal mechanism. If you can accept that premise, we can move to the next level—the creature itself.

"While on a dig in the shadow of Borneo's Mt. Kinabalu, my research team found traces of the same DNA our Haitian medical partners found in the dead boy. Not close, not similar, not sort of like. Same! Identical. No question. We found this DNA in bones. Bones from some odd, ancient creature. Most of those bones are now being subjected to rigorous investigation and analysis at the University of Wisconsin and elsewhere. As you might expect, some of the bone specimens were forwarded to the Atlanta laboratories of the Centers of Disease Control, too.

"Before you form an incorrect assumption, let me explain that the Haitian boy did not attain this so-called *condition* from our dig at Mount Kinabalu. The Borneo find is far too recent to have been the cause. Frankly, I do not know where the boy acquired it. My theory is that it had something to do with the earthquake. That quake may have opened up some chasm on the island, some ancient, fossilized bones that contained the same … well, for the lack of a better term, *spore*. Someday we may know the answers. Right now, here, tonight, we don't need to know where it came from as much as where it is going, how fast it will spread, and what options exist for those afflicted.

"So. What do we know thus far? We know a boy is dead. We know we found some bones—bones with DNA identical to that found in the same dead Haitian boy. When that poor, little Haitian boy died, his corpse had growing inside what I believe to be a far-distant descendent of the creature whose bones we found in Borneo. It is not a named creature as yet. I was hoping to have it named after me. I have changed my mind. I don't want my name associated with this thing. It is a quadruped, reptilian in appearance. A carnivore. Probably a predator. Big. How big? Think Volkswagen big. Volkswagen van big.

"Regarding the case in Haiti, I estimate the creature had been gestating in the boy for over a year. This small, rather malnourished boy was simply not healthy enough to continue the gestation. He was literally eaten alive from the inside out. I believe, had the boy not died, the creature could have completed its gestation and, in time, been born. I am confident when I say the gestation period of this animal would have been somewhere between four and ten years. My U of Chicago colleagues concur.

"The creature, this parasitic invader, grows very slowly. So slowly that the host—the human host—does not realize what is happening, other than what appears to be unwanted, yet normal, weight gain over time. Eventually, the creature will have to exit the host. Because we have not seen this gestation carried to term, there is no way of knowing what avenue the creature will take upon exit. We do know, based on the boy's experience, that it will be around thirty to forty pounds, possibly more. I doubt many human hosts will survive giving birth to these … things.

"Other information I am able to share at this time is that the creature's outer shell appears to be clad with heavy scales. It has a round, horned head, short neck, long tail. Its claws are not unlike those of a snapping turtle, well-suited for ripping flesh from bone.

"I am certain that, by now, the CDC has far more information, but you know as well as I do, the CDC is very unlikely to share that information for a variety of reasons. Personally, I feel word of this should be freely circulated as soon as possible. Time, as they say, is of the essence. The public needs to learn of this now. It is, in my personal opinion, every human's right to know. I only hope news of this does not result in widespread panic—world panic.

"I would like to offer you more. I cannot. At this time, however, my best advice to the general public is to step on the bathroom scale. Anyone noticing weight gain, *any* weight gain over the last, say, one to five years, should immediately contact the family physician. Get a referral for a sonogram, X-ray, or both. Depending on those results, it might be prudent to immediately arrange for a surgeon to do the extraction. Individuals here tonight may wish to do this in the very near future, as I am certain the health insurance carriers will soon be bankrupt when millions upon millions of afflicted patients start knocking on their doors. At that point, all those who cannot pay will be faced with carrying the creature's gestation to term, a sight I hope never to see. I suppose, like the mother of the Haitian boy, suicide might become a popular option. Let us hope not."

I folded my notes, removed my reading glasses, and stuffed both in the pocket of my lab coat saying, "That, ladies and gentlemen, concludes my presentation. I am Professor Charles Watersteen-Dragg and I thank you for your time and the opportunity to speak tonight. Are there any questions?"

New Neighbors

On a moonlit night of yore,
Your town did a werewolf explore.
It ate all the rats
And the neighborhood cats,
And now it's moved in right next door.

Dragon Breath

Somewhere in your gut there resides
A dragon. Deep down there he hides.
So, know when you pass
Malodorous gas,
'Tis dragon breath from your insides.

In Gloomy Wood

In a gloomy wood, astray,
Insanely flound'ring with no aim,
Numbed from drink, in deep dismay,
I wandered sleepless, deep in pain.
While mourning deeply for my love,
Weeping for my lost Lorraine,
An angel swept down from above,
Calling out my name.
Calling out, then saying,

"Tears you shed for your fair love,
Agony from her dark death,
All the grief that comes thereof
From shame, sir, you must claim."
"Messenger," I did explain,
"I deeply loved this one now slain!
Leave me to my aimless pain,
Pain for lost Lorraine,
My love now lost, Lorraine."

"Accuse me not. I'm not to blame.
'Twas not me who forged the knife.
'Twas not me who, with disdain,
Took my lover's life!

"No! Not me, who from the mist,
Brought this grief, caused this strife,
Wrought the blade that deadly twist
Slaying my young wife.
My sweet, young, gentle wife."

"Surely, you must know this well,
Looking down from high above,
I'm not the one whom she did tell,
Of her other love."

"'Twas not me who, wild from mead,
Into that pit, her corpse did shove,
Accuse me not of this foul deed.
I slew not my love.
My sweet, young, gentle love."

“’Twas not me who threw her down,
Who buried her in shallow pit,
Far beyond the gleam of town
Where the fields do seem to quit.”

“There, where she can see the moon
Shine down bright where roads do split,
Below the mount where lovers spoon,
The mount that’s now moonlit.
That lover’s mount, moonlit”

The angel then showed badge and face.
He snatched the drink that fogged my brain.
Shackles soon secured my place,
Still, I mourned my sweet Lorraine.

’Twas no angel from above,
Who did, in gloomy wood, obtain
Proof of who did kill my love.
Proof I was to blame.
And alone I bear that shame.

Now, imprisoned, in dismay,
Insanely wailing without aim,
Through gloomy wood, I long to stray.
Stray steeped with dread, deep in pain.
    Now mourning, sleepless for my love,
    Mourning for my lost Lorraine,
    The hangman soon will, from above,
    Be calling out my name.
    Yes, calling out my name.

'Tis then I'll join my sweet Lorraine.
Night and day, without dismay,
We'll wander free, devoid of pain.
Stay we will in gloomy wood,
    In a gloomy wood, astray.

Thief of Dreams VI

Stealing dreams is no state crime, they say.
Yet, a thief's a thief, my friend, come what may.
The window soon will close
Know you must absorb all those
Frightful dreams that lay along your way.

Delightful tales so dark and so sublime
Await you now, voyeur friend of mine.
They turn and twist
Like hangmen's victims in the mist.
Soak in these words now yours that once were mine.

Still do keep your lamp turned way down low
As across the ages we now go.

Death Deceived

On pale horse, Death waits for us
Down every trail we tread.
No cheating, no defeating his dark deed.
No exemption that I know,
’Cept one from long ago.
A freakish tale from old, indeed unique.
A tale you may find truly oblique.

In the day of Lionheart,
A brave and noble knight,
Sword in hand, for holy land did ‘light.
As he came to English sea,
Death and Devil came to he,
Hoping for his soul that dreary night.
Craving for his soul ’fore morning’s light.

Death held high his hour glass,
There for Knight to see,
Sand quickly flowing, showing fleeting time.
“Know, good knight, there is no cheating,
No avoiding, no defeating,
No muffling of the church bell’s final chime.
No muffling of the final bell sublime.

"For, if you venture 'cross this sea
To fight your noble fight,
And leave behind your precious English loam,
You'll ne'er returneth here.
Nor again see mornings clear
From this beloved land you now do roam.
You'll perish far from cherished land called home.

"But, should you stay, I'll stay your death,
Delay a thousand years,
And Satan? Your soul he will never see.
A coward's badge will be your pay.
So choose now, fight or stay.
English soil or toil across the sea?
Precious soil or glory 'cross the sea?"

"Say once more," this champion said,
"If I ne'er leave home behind,
One thousand years more I'll have on your glass?
And Heaven's gate I'll surely see?
Are these the words you say to me?
Heaven after one full-thousand pass?"
Death said, "Heaven when one thousand annum pass."

Off he rode, our gallant knight,
To fight the noble fight,
To carry Cross across the holy land.
Brave and bold, he wielded sword,
Then a vessel he did board,
Sailing home to claim his earned reward.
Returning to his land and sweet reward.

Back home in glory, our knight sought
A word with old man Death.
"I've returned. Now my prize I take.
One thousand years you said,
And Heaven's gentle bed,
If English soil I did not forsake.
And my home, Sir, I did not forsake."

Taking then, from 'round his neck,
A simple silver vial,
Our champion poured into outstretched hand,
Earth from his garden fair,
His English garden where
He had gathered up its loamy sand.
Before he left he'd gathered loamy sand.
And still this champion rides across his land.
For centuries more he'll ride 'cross cherished land.

Beyond the Laterals

I'm Wilber Watson. Feel free to call me Will. I've worked animal control for the health department for nearly thirty years and I have never seen anything like this. Never.

Snakes in our sewers? Sure! There is not one city in the country, or the continent for that matter, that does not have snakes in its sewers. Ever since the pet shops started offering snakes to their customers in the nineteen thirties, we've had snakes in the sewers. Snakes, guppies, goldfish, gators, geckos, you name it. Lord knows what else. Systems designed for the removal and treatment of human waste have now become disposal facilities for society's unwanted pets and whatever else people throw down their damn drains.

Yeah, we have snakes in the sewers—have for years. No problem. No problem until now. That damn ordinance rammed through the legislature by the state health department changed everything. Some multi-phobic jerk in the state capital decided he did not want snakes in the sewers. Never mind that those snakes didn't hurt a soul or cause any problems. In fact, they kept the rat population down. Now, since this new law took effect, not only do we also have these damn snakes to deal with, we have more rats coming out of the sewer grates, into our yards, and our homes. Rats and snakes. Just what I need after thirty years in animal control!

Well, by now you've probably heard the rest of the

story—how some herpetologist the Public Health Department came up with that lame-brained, terrible *snake*-icide chemical that drove the snakes crazy—how the snakes reacted by finding the easiest way out—how they found their way upstream through the mains, beyond the laterals, through the sewer lines, into the household waste pipes. That's where the real problem began. You see, for all but the largest snakes, the anacondas and pythons, it was a quick slither through the toilet trap and into the bowl. There, they found fresh water—pesticide-free water. All they needed then was a place to hide. They found it—right under the rim. Right under the rim where they can remain concealed all day, avoiding direct light until dark when they go on the prowl for food.

Now you know why the State Health Department is issuing those long-handled inspection mirrors to all citizens. The telescopic handles stretch far enough so the user has less chance of getting bitten when checking under the rim. Yes, I know it's a bother. So were seat belts. And, as you know, some folks use seat belts and survive crashes, some don't use them and die. Same deal with the snakes and the mirrors—some folks—most folks—will get into the habit of inspecting under the rim. The rest? Well, you can figure it out for yourself.

I've worked in animal control for thirty years. That's enough. I can't deal with this. I just cleaned out my desk and turned in my resignation. I have had enough.

The Bullet: Two-thousandths of a Second

has been removed from this collection in respect for readers who have experienced trauma, mental or physical, from violent acts involving guns.

The poem was deemed by the author to be too graphic for some readers. It is available in digital format only by special request from the publisher. The price of this book reflects the absence of this poem.

BadgerValley.com

The Zombie Apocalypse

Part IV

Willie Dancier lay face down, stone-cold dead when Detective Terry Hampton found him in the basement storeroom of Moxie's. He found Willie, but no flasks of the kid's formula. He phoned his partner. It would take a team to thoroughly search the club for the nano-biotic solution.

"Back-up just arrived, Terry," came the voice through his phone. "Sergeant Wilson and three of his men are entering the front of the building right now. Richardson and Hobbs will cover the alley in case anyone sneaks out the back door. I'm coming in with two patrolmen now."

"Logan," Hampton replied, "Willie Dancier's dead. Blood all over down here. Tell Hobbs to get the forensics team photographer down here as soon as possible. We need photos before we can tear this place apart. We gotta find those four liters of the kid's solution."

"Roger that, Terry."

Within minutes, the SFPD forensics unit had photographed the scene and returned to the corpse in the alley. Hampton rolled Willie Dancier onto his back, bringing a chorus of gasps from the remaining officers. The flesh from Dancier's face was missing. Lips, nose, cheeks, chin—torn from the skull and gone. Blood-filled sockets had replaced eyes. Without flesh, the gruesome, bloody skull seemed to grin at those who stared down in disgusted disbelief.

Logan Quimby forced words from his gullet. “My God, Terry, why would anyone do this? Who …”

“Not who, Logan—it’s a question of what. That corpse in the alley was not human. At least it was not human when we dispatched it. Remember what that grad student told us? Increased appetite for meat protein and altered brain function. Looks like the kid created a bona fide monster, here. Hollywood couldn’t have done better.”

“Detective Hampton?” came an officer’s voice from the next room. “We found twenty-two vials of something here.”

“Twenty-two? Okay. Twenty-two. That’s a start. Get it to the lab techs. Logan, the kid said there was enough for a thousand vials. We’ve probably seen the results of one vial here tonight.” He pulled his ringing phone from his pocket. “Hampton here.”

“Detective, the chief and the coroner just arrived. They’re standin’ next to the stiff in the alley and want some answers.”

“Yes, I imagine they do. Okay. I’ll try to fill ’em in. Tell ’em I’m on my way.” He turned to his partner. “Logan, you damn-well better back me up. I gave that thing up there in the alley a kill-shot in the head and I don’t want to lose my damn badge over it. Jesus! Just look at the mess that kid has created! Logan, what is this city going to do to protect its people from these godawful things?”

Hampton pocketed his phone and stepped closer to Willie Dancier's corpse as he stretched a latex glove over his left hand. He checked Willie's back pockets, pulling out a black wallet thick with hundred-dollar bills. A slip of paper bearing notes scribbled in pencil fell from the wallet into the half-coagulated blood below. Hampton picked it up and was wiping it on Willie's sleeve when he heard the dispatch. "All units. All units. Disturbance at 756 Union Street between Powell and Mason. Multiple suspects reported to be eating dead body. All units ..."

Four SFPD officers raced up the steps and into the alley. The detectives followed. Hampton walked straight to the SFPD Chief of Police and pointed to the dead body. "Sir, this may not be the best time for a chat. You're looking at the corpse of a crazed cannibal there—a monster. Not human. You heard dispatch. It sounds like there's a group of these things eating some dead guy down by Washington Park right now. Okay, now look at this."

Terry Hampton handed the slip of paper to his boss. Scribbled on the blood-stained note were, NYC 300, CHI 200, LA 200, DAL 100 .... The list continued.

"If my hunch is right, the drug that created this thing is on its way to dealers across the country and there's over sixty vials in the Bay area to account for. Sir, Quimby and I will track 'em down. You might want to get on the phone with these other cities and Homeland Security, Chief. I think the grad student that created this … this nano-bot formula may have started ..."

"Started what, Detective?"

"Sir, I think the media called it … the Zombie Apocalypse."

In the basement of the Moxie Club, Willie Dancier's corpse jerked violently as its heart resumed beating. Filled with acute pangs from hunger, it gasped a deep, spasmodic, rasping breath and struggled to its feet, turning toward the steps leading to the alley.

Move Not Cold Stones by Midnight's Mist

How putrid hung the vapours, thick and green,
When Lord and Lady crossed the garden gate
And there inhaled this hideous mist obscene.
Quite fatal was their foolish tempt of fate.

Old monuments for those who'd long been dead,
These headstones, he had moved far from the house,
So flowers could be planted in their staid,
A garden of delight for Lord and spouse.

What wond'rous gifts came from this garden fair,
Most marv'lous blooms, so sweet with love's perfume,
Till deadly, rotten vapours fouled the air,
Angered spirit's mist in light of moon.

Before you move a headstone, do beware.
Lest you next add green stench to midnight air.

Thief of Dreams VII

And so, a Thief of Dreams you've now become.
Oh, dear one,
I fear you've just begun
A journey down life's darkest dreary track.
No, don't turn back.
Behind you there is no salvation.
A voyeur are you now
Of nightmares. Oh, and how
You'll long crave even darker tales than these.

The nightmares of the drunkard are now yours,
But just beyond stand many other doors,
Many other evil dreams,
Chilling, shivery screams
From those tormented ghouls that man abhors.

And if your nightmares have not by now begun,
Perhaps, dear voyeur, turn backward to page one.
And, when your explorations here are through,
Oh, Thief of Dreams, consider volume two.
A volume darkly crafted just for you.

Pleasant dreams,

James A. Brakken

About the author

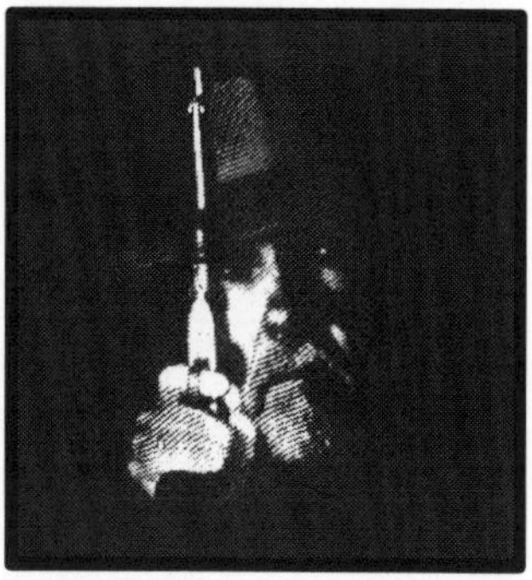

James A. Brakken likes a good scary story now and then. He enjoys writing them, too. Every poem and short story within these pages is original, created in one summer's time, between two of the author's Tor Loken series novels. The graphics, however took longer. They are the work of great masters of art—etchings and engravings that date back centuries.

Bar the door, secure the windows, close the blinds, and experience DARK, a delightfully frightful journey through the bizarre recesses of fear.

Thank you for reporting to the author any errors you may find in DARK and THE TREASURE OF NAMAKAGON so future editions of these books may be improved.

Find us on Facebook® If you enjoy DARK or THE TREASURE OF NAMAKAGON, please *like* us on Facebook®. Let your friends know, too!

Looking for Treasure?

Get sneak peeks of THE TREASURE OF NAMAKAGON, the accompanying study and discussion guide, plus maps, new engraved illustrations, and much more. Visit our website TheTreasureofNamakagon.com or BadgerValley.com for more information about the great 19th century timber harvest in northern Wisconsin and the ongoing search for Chief Namakagon's lost treasure.

Publish *YOUR* Book!

Visit BadgerValley.com to learn how easy and inexpensive publishing can be. Cookbooks, family histories, how-to books, novels and everything in between can be published in softcover or ebooks or both. You provide the manuscript in standard digital format, we do the rest.

The DARK Illustratons are etchings and engravings from master artists of long ago. They are in public domain and available for public use, free from copyright. A list of the artists whose work appears in DARK is available at BadgerValley.com

Watch for the next book in the Tor Loken series .....

Tor Loken and the Death of Namakagon

According to mid-1880s articles found in the Ashland Daily Press, Chief Namakagon traded unrefined silver for supplies and services in Ashland. Several area businessmen tried to convince the chief to disclose the source of his silver. None did, although one, it's been said, came very close. However, when a large bear blocked the trail, Namakagon took this for a bad omen, refusing to continue. Following a fierce 1886 blizzard, Namakagon's frozen remains were found along a trail many believe was very near his silver cache. Suspicions remain today regarding his demise and of the whereabouts of the lost silver cache.

In the next adventure, Tor Loken loses his mentor during this fierce snowstorm. The authorities refuse to investigate and Tor is challenged to solve the mystery of Chief Namakagon's death. Meanwhile, new developments, both man-made and nature-made, again place the Loken camp in peril.

Learn more about the rich history of the lumberjack days, gather more clues about the likely location of the legendary silver mine, and help Tor Loken solve the mystery surrounding the death of Chief Namakagon.

Available now at the finest indy bookstores, many historical museums and at BadgerValley.com ....

The Treasure of Namakagon

A young lumberjack, his Ojibwe mentor, and the treasure, yet to be rediscovered.

Based on 19th century "lumberjack" histories from northwestern Wisconsin, this action-adventure will place the reader in the midst of the great lumber camps or on the spring log drive down the Namekagon River or in town for a Saturday night of revelry and brawling with rival camps. The references to lumberjack life, fraudulent timber sales, and big woods violence resulting in gunplay are all founded on true events, as are the accounts of silver and gold found in the northwestern Wisconsin and Chief Namakagon's treasure. Although many still search for the secret silver mine, it has yet to be rediscovered. Perhaps, though, the real treasure was the vast white pine forest that, until the 1880s, gave Wisconsin its character, its life.

TREASURE will plunge you into Wisconsin's single, greatest economic event—the post-Civil War harvest of the largest stand of white pine in the world. Estimates said that timber would take a thousand years to cut. It was gone in just fifty. Tens upon tens of thousands of lumberjacks descended on the lawless north country to harvest the "green gold" and cash in on the wealth. Many northern Wisconsin towns sprang up in the middle of nowhere and boomed into bustling cities full of life, fast money, fortune seekers, loose women, and lumberjacks. Rowdy wilderness towns quickly gained popularity—and notoriety. Most are now gone, along with the great men who came to Wisconsin's pinery with only a dream.

This action-packed adventure is based on those great men and the hard but colorful lives they lived. This story is also based on the history of Mikwam-migwan, better known as Chief Namakagon, and his legendary lost treasure.

Step back in time. Share in the rich history of life in the great Wisconsin pinery during the lumberjack days of the 1880s. Share, too, in a great, twisting, turning, spellbinding north woods adventure.

It's all within THE TREASURE OF NAMAKAGON, 247 pages, 43 chapters and 63 illustrations by James A. Brakken.

Reader's comments regarding THE TREASURE OF NAMAKAGON:

"Weaving mystery into history, "The Treasure of Namakagon" vivifies the tumultuous nature of 19th-century life in the legendary north woods."

Michael Perry, bestselling Wisconsin author

"I enjoyed reading his novel. It's pretty accurate history."

Larry Meiller, Wisconsin Public Radio host

"Open with caution. You won't want to put this one down."

LaMoine MacLaughlin, President,
Wisconsin Writers Association

"A twisting, thrilling mix of mystery, adventure and legendary treasure. ...a great fund raising idea for our lake associations. Wisconsin history buffs will find this book a treasure in itself. An exciting adventure for all ages."

Waldo Asp, Northwest Waters President and AARP County Chairman

"Like a living history lesson, Brakken takes his readers on a ride down northern Wisconsin's untamed Namakagon River, back when giant virgin forests lured heroic lumberjacks to seek their fortune. In scene after scene, the reader is surrounded by the beauty of pristine woods and lakes, rooting for the good guys to beat out the greedy ones, even learning step by step how to place the giant saw so the magnificent tree falls in just the right place."

A.Y. Stratton, author of Buried Heart

Print & order DARK & The Treasure of Namakagon

A twisting, turning, thrilling adventure based on records from the great Wisconsin timber boom of the 1880s. Tor Loken and his mentor, Chief Namakagon, join with lumberjacks from their camp to foil a ruthless timber tycoon and protect the secret silver, treasure that truly existed and has yet to be rediscovered.

Discussion & Study Guide to accompany THE TREASURE OF NAMAKAGON. 186 questions & projects to help readers reach an in-depth understanding of the story and the rich history of the 19th century Wisconsin timber harvest. Ideal for classrrom* & discussion groups.

DARK James A. Brakken's original eerie poetry and delightfully frightful stories.

Item	Price	Quantity	Extended Price
Treasure of Namakagon	$15.99		___.__
'TREASURE' Study Guide Study Gd + Ansr Key*	$3.99 $10.99		___.__ ___.__
DARK (Includes Dark, Darker & Darkest)	$17.99		___.__
S & H in USA: $4 first item, $1 each add'l item			___.__
US dollars only. 6% sales tax if shipped to WI address			___.__
Please provide your email for delivery confirmation: Total *Prices subject to change without notice.* Questions? 715-798-3163 or BayfieldCountyLakes@Yahoo.com			$ ___.__

*Free study guide & key with 10 or more books.

Mail entire form & check or money order payable to:
James A. Brakken
45255 E. Cable Lk. Rd
Cable, WI 54821
Email: BayfieldCountyLakes@Yahoo.com

Find e-book versions for all e-readers atTheTreasureofNamakagon.com

For online orders, visit
BadgerValley.com

Brakken's TREASURE OF NAMAKAGON
45255 East Cable Lake Road
Cable WI 54821

Name ____________________

Address ____________________

City/State/Zip ____________________

*THIS IS YOUR **SHIPPING LABEL**: PLEASE PRINT CLEARLY*

About DARK

Imagine you are a mind reader—a voyeur who can steal dreams. In DARK, you will immediately become "The Thief of Dreams," allowing you to purloin well over 50 dreadful, occasionally humorous, and sometimes downright disturbing dreams, fantasies, and nightmares of others. All are expressed as poetry and short stories, each designed to make you laugh or cringe or both.

For example, all four parts of "The Zombie Apocalypse" series drew that title from a recent admission by Google® that this was their most-searched term in June, 2012. Many believe the Z A will happen. Brakken explains, in his Z A series, that, thanks to recent scientific innovation, this idea, this threat, is, indeed, plausible. Those who initially thought this term laughable may find themselves reconsidering. As we all know, science can be wonderful—or terrible—depending on the final product.

Poems such as "In Gloomy Wood" and "The Parson Joshua Black" tell stories that will tingle the spine. Others like "Something in the Shadows" and "Bedtime Story" may lead to the bedroom light left on until morning. "Gramma's Noggin" will elicit a laugh while helping readers pronounce Namakagon correctly. A sonnet, "The Count," will beg readers for restraint regarding releasing evil upon the land.

Brakken included "Nevermore" a poetic tribute to Edgar Allen Poe, a favorite of many. "Nevermore" answers Poe's question about the final resting place of the spirit of the deceased maiden in Poe's, "The Raven."

A number of poems, including "The Ballad of Ole Johnson" and "A Pinery Tale" found inspiration in actual deaths that occurred during northern Wisconsin's 19th century timber harvest, giving them the western texture akin to the cowboy poetry of Baxter Black. Several mysterious excerpts from Brakken's 19th century "lumberjack" era novel, THE TREASURE OF NAMAKAGON, complement the poems nicely. And, if dragons are to your liking, you'll savor the author's "Three Dragons" series.

Beware! Although this large collection of Brakken's macabre writings will delightfully scare the reader and sometimes stimulate laughter, the author advises us that some of these works are utterly disturbing.

Perhaps that is why, for visual relief, the author included 53 darkly evocative engravings by master artists from ancient times. Gustave Dore and Albrecht Durer are among the artists who, long after their death, add mystery and macabre charm to Brakken's work. **Note that these images are not intended to illustrate the writings. Rather, they simply add to the enigmatic, bone-chilling nature of DARK.**

THE AUTHOR ADVISES READING DARK AS PRESENTED.
Jumping ahead may spoil the twisting, turning plots of some sequential works.
Sneak peeks of both DARK and THE TREASURE OF NAMAKAGON are at

Badger Valley Publishing   BadgerValley.com

Read what the DARK, DARKER & DARKEST critics say:

From the ghost of Mary Shelly, **"James A. Brakken's has created DARK, an eerie, often humorous assembly of tales and poems. DARK is a creature far more loveable than that of my dear Dr. Frankenstein. Why, *it's alive* with fun!"**

"Damnation! Brakken's DARK is one helluva good read!" *Ghost of John Milton, author of Paradise Lost*

"Only since reading Brakken's DARK collection, do I find myself wearing a wreath of garlic and carrying a crucifix on my travels—just in case!" *The ghost of Bram Stoeker*

From the Invisible Man, **"Thankfully, I was able to see my way clear to getting a copy of DARK!**

"DARK is a howling good read. One might say I simply devoured it!" *The ghost of Larry Talbot, aka Wolf Man*

From the ghost of the Mummy, **"Curse upon mortals who have not read DARK. Yeeesh! Brakken's writing really creeps me out, dude!"**

"As I ponder, weary, in my chamber dreary, wouldst I be without James A. Brakken's DARK book? Nevermore!" *The ghost of Edgar Allen Poe*

"My story, "The Willows," was creepy, yes, but never this much fun!" *The ghost of Algernon Blackwood*

"Egad! Had a copy of James Brakken's DARK been sequestered within the withering, musty walls of my seven-gabled house, its leaves would have had my characters drunk from its lively and various spirits!" *The ghost of Nathanial Hawthorn*

"Since reading DARK, the residents of Sleepy Hollow get little sleep." *The ghost of Washington Irving*

Finally, from Satan, himself, **"When I hear of a soul who does not have a copy of DARK, well, let's just say it really burns me up!"**

Badger Valley Publishing ***BadgerValley.com***

14626605R50110

Made in the USA
Charleston, SC
25 September 2012